# THE THRONE II

COLE HART

**CONTENTS**

**The Throne II**



Published in the United States of America.



Published by Cole Hart Signature, LLC.

**Mailing List**

**To stay up to date on new releases, plus get information on contests, sneak peeks, and more,**

***Go To The Website Below...***

**www.colehartsignature.com**

## BOOKS BY COLE HART:

I'm Just Tryin' To Be Somebody's Wife

The Sunday School Teacher

The Sunday school Teacher II

I Need A Fiancée Like Beyonce

I Like My Women BBW

Rich Thugs

The Throne

The Throne 2

The Throne 3

The Throne 4

The Plug

The Plug 2

Godfather of Atlanta

Godfather of Atlanta 2

Red Bottom Bitches

Red Bottom Bitches 2

Red Bottom Bitches 3

Drunk In Love: An Original Love Story

Drunk In Love 2: An Original Love Story

Drunk In Love 3: An Original Love Story

Drunk In Love 4: An Original Love Story

Crazy Summer

Bow Tie Mafia

Bow Tie Mafia 2

Bankroll Squad Augusta

Street Advocate

A-Town Veteran

This Summer Is Lit

I'm Low Key Feeling You

I'm Low Key Feeling You 2: The Finale

## CONTACT THE AUTHOR:

Facebook: Cole Hart
Facebook Author Page: Author Cole Hart
Instagram: @authorcolehart

*The Throne 2 is dedicated to the memory of:*

*Frank Johnson*

*9/18/1928 – 12/17/2012*

## THE CONVERSATION

When I pulled up in front of my old man's house, I put my foot on the brake and came to a complete stop. I took a deep breath, because I was desperately trying to shake my nervousness away. Damn. I hadn't seen him in nearly fifteen years, and that was mainly because I went to prison way back in 99. Now I was home, and I was definitely ready to settle the minor dispute that we had had years ago over the phone.

I checked myself in the rearview mirror. Real clean, debonair. White teeth, fresh shave. Then I looked over my attire. Blue Gators on my feet. Designer jeans, linen shirt underneath my leather jacket. I took another deep breath, looking at the house again, and my heart began to thump harder. I finally eased the car in park and switched off the engine.

On the floor in the back seat I had a copy of every book that I had written while I was in prison. They were all inside the leather Michael Kors bag. I reached behind the seat and grabbed the strap, pulled it forward, and slung it over my shoulder. When I stepped out, I eased my platinum Cartier's on my face immediately and walked up a short flight of red brick steps and pressed the illuminated door bell.

It wasn't long before I heard the locks being removed from the inside. When the door came open, I froze. Only for a few seconds, though. The eighty plus year old Warrior balanced himself on a wooden cane, we stared each other in the eyes for what seemed like forever. I moved up on the screened in front porch. The old man was short, standing five six and gray haired. I put my arms around his shoulders and his slipped underneath mine.

We held on to each other for a few minutes, then he led me through the front door and inside the small cozy living room. There was a double stuffed leather sofa, love seat and a chair. He went straight to the chair and carefully took his seat.

"Sit down, man." he said to me.

I removed the leather bag from my shoulder and found a seat on the loveseat. Looking around the strange and unfamiliar place, I didn't know where to start with the conversation. I finally allowed my eyes to settle in on him. "It's been fifteen years since we seen each other. How you been doing?"

"Still making it. Lil cold, every now and then." He paused and touched his chest. "Still strong as an Ox."

I smiled at that, and nodded my head at the same time. I unzipped the Michael Kors duffel bag and pulled a few paperback books out. I handed him a copy of Crazy Summer.

He pulled a pair of glasses from his shirt pocket and eased them on his face. He looked at the cover with a slight frown. "Who is Cole Hart"

"That's me."

"I don't remember that name," he said.

I laughed. "Just my pen name."

He grunted, stared at the cover from front to back. Then his eyes cut back up at me. "You wrote this in prison?"

I smiled, then nodded with confidence and pride. I reached

into the bag again and came out with a copy of A-Town Veteran and The Throne 1&2. I handed those to him as well.

He took them and examined them also. “This good, real good. At least you didn't waste yo time in there.”

At that moment, I could only nod my head, thinking hard to myself. Over the years, I had so many questions that I’d wanted to ask him. Now here I was, feeling as if everything was alright. But I was angry with him. A Father I Never Knew. At least that’s what I thought.

He caught me staring in space. Then he said, “Go ahead, get it out.”

His statement caught me off guard, as if he was reading my mind or something. I finally eased up to the edge of the loveseat and took another deep breath, trying to relax myself. He was looking at the cover of The Throne. His eyes were fixed on the gold plated .45’s.

“You shouldn't wanna see another gun.”

Then I hit him with the first question.

“Why we never had a chance to bond? You know, father son relationship.”

The living room fell silent. I watched him push his glasses further up on his face. His eyes settled on mine, long and hard. “In life, a man has to make decisions. A father has to make decisions. A husband has to make decisions. And sometimes those decisions may not benefit everyone, and everyone won't agree with your final decision.” He paused, then he went on. “I’m sure you know that I was married when you was born.”

“Definitely,” I said to him. “I figured that much out.”

“In this world, the real world. Life isn’t easy by a long shot.”

“And I was that long shot.”

“Naw, you was a blessing.”

The old man caught me off guard with that one. Now I definitely knew he was a man of God, the man went to church every Sunday that I could remember. Coming through in that blue Cadillac and stepping out in his three-piece suit. *Damn. That was every Sunday for real.*

"Did you hear me?"

I was back in the eighties, lost in thought. He brought me back. "A blessing?" I asked him.

"A blessing," He said again. "It was a lot of things I wanted to do, but under the circumstances, I couldn't. It was probably out of fear of me losing everything I'd built and worked for. That goes back to the decisions a man has to make in life. I'm sure you've made several decisions in life that a lot of people didn't agree with."

I looked at him, allowing his words to register, sink all the way into my soul. It's funny how things could be explained in so many ways. A grown man conversation, one that would make me think harder.

"Prime example," he said. "You became a father at sixteen. Was you ready?"

"Yeah, I didn't have a choice."

"But you got locked up a month later after she was born. You was gone two years."

"I was hustling in the streets then."

"That goes back to the decisions that we make as men, fathers and husbands."

I sat back on the love seat, rubbed my hand downward over my mustache and my mouth. I crossed my legs and looked him in his eyes. Words of wisdom were good for the soul. Then I saw him wipe a falling tear from his sagging cheek. "But what you didn't know, is that I filled your shoes. I made sure she was good."

"And I really appreciate that. However, I still believe that my life would've turned out differently if I could've gotten that guidance from you."

"And I do agree, and that was something I ask you to forgive me for."

“I forgive you. Straight like that, because I didn't think you would give it to me like this. I had many restless nights in that prison cell thinking about this day.”

“Not a day nor night went by without me praying for you. Through it all, that was the only way I was connected to you. Spiritually I've always been there.”

After another long silence, I could feel the tears trying to push their way forward. I stopped breathing for two seconds then forced a smile to really keep from crying tears of joy. “I never looked at it that way,” I said.

“Are you a God fearing man?”

I nodded my head, and loud and clear, I responded, “Definitely.”

“Well enough said, then.”

He made a fist, brought it up to his mouth, and began coughing uncontrollably, rocking back and forth.

I stood up and moved over towards him. My hand on his back, I bent over slightly where my face was only inches from his. I patted his back. “You alright? You need something to drank?”

He coughed twice more, and slowly shook his head side -to-side. Then he breathed heavy. His chest rising and falling. I sat down on the arm of the chair and placed my hand on his right shoulder, his hand rested on top of mine. He was in an emotional state, and I was also.

He finally looked up at me. “I'll be alright.” His words sounded weaker now, as if they were echoing from a cave. I could hear the sound of a train and the scent of fresh cut flowers began filling my nostrils.

“Come get me Sunday, we'll go to church together.”

I stood up, gave him a hand, and he came up to. We faced off, and I wrapped my arms around him. He hugged me back, and whispered. “I'll always love you, son.”

~

When my eyes parted open, I looked around the small and dark prison cell and realized that I was in a deep dream. I stared around in pure darkness and my heart was beating fast as if it was about to jump out of my chest. Fidgety is the way I was feeling, but it was a good fidgety. I didn't want to wake my cellmates up, so I quietly slipped out of my bunk and eased my feet into a pair of Nike slippers. I placed my hand on the cold concrete wall and fell to one knee and said my morning prayer. After I finished praying, I brushed my teeth and washed my face

*Man, go call yo old man.* I told myself. I looked at myself in the mirror and removed my wave cap. I checked my watch and it read 8:17 AM. I pressed the button and the cell door popped open. I walked out into the dormitory feeling good about the dream that I just had about my old man. It was deep, and I was ready to make the peace. You know, let go and let God type of situation. There were four separate blue phones on the wall. I grabbed the first one and punched in my wife's number so she could call him on three way for me.

The operator said what she had to say, and a moment later, I heard my wife's voice come through the phone.

"Hey," Was all she said.

For some reason, she just didn't sound right to me. So the first thing I asked was, "What's wrong?"

She hesitated. "You talked to ya sistah?"

"Last week. Why?"

Another long silence, then she broke the news to me. "Your daddy."

My lips tightened, I froze. My eyes didn't blink, and my heart had sunk into the pit of my stomach. I finally built my nerves and asked her. "What about him?"

"God took him this morning, baby."

I couldn’t respond, it felt as if someone had taken my heart from my chest and tore it into tiny painful pieces that made me cringe with every second. I released the phone and it bounced off the wall until it finally stopped moving. I leaned against the wall and slowly slid down until I was sitting on the floor.

I buried my face in my hands, thinking hard as tears flooded my face. I couldn't help it, no matter how hard I tried. And all I could think was, *I never had a chance to say I love you.*

# PROLOGUE

Falisa's bedroom at the sanitarium was tastefully decorated with handcrafted furniture. Her floor was black marble, with hand-frescoed walls on all four sides, and no windows. Resting peacefully in her colossal mahogany four-poster bed, she was disturbed by the annoying buzzing from one of her three smart phones that were charging on the nightstand next to her. Surrounded by total darkness, she lay in her bed with her eyes still closed. The Egyptian cotton sheets felt cool and comfortable against her skin. The phone was still buzzing, but she wasn't about to answer it.

Falisa took a long, deep breath when the phone finally stopped buzzing. She carefully turned over on her side and pulled the sheet up to her neck. With another deep breath, she was finally relaxing again. Then the phone buzzed yet another time. Falisa sucked her teeth. *Shit.* She turned over and faced the nightstand. She picked up the ringing phone and noticed a 305 area code, but the number was unfamiliar to her. *A Miami number.*

She answered, and what she heard from the other end gave her a surge of energy; even more than an adrenaline rush.

"Mataste a mi hermano perra, te voy a matar a ti y a toda tu familia."

The words came in a deep, thick Spanish accent.

Falisa flipped the sheets back and carefully sat up. She swung her feet out of bed, with the phone still pressed against the side of her face. "Respect it or check it," she politely said. She took a deep breath and went on with the rest of her sentence. "And first you got to find me, bitch."

Falisa calmly ended the call, then she studied the number. She tattooed it on her memory cell. "Muthafuckin' Colombians think I'm something to play with," she mumbled under her breath. She picked up another phone on the stand. She pressed a number for speed dial. Someone answered immediately. The voice greeted Falisa in a French accent, and she responded back in Swahili, then she switched it up to Pig Latin. The conversation only lasted five minutes after Falisa gave the person on the other end, the 305 phone number that had just called her. She hung up, and then pressed a button on the wall that went to her nurse's room.

"Are you eating breakfast this morning, sweetheart?" Falisa asked into the intercom.

The nurse's voice came back through the intercom. "Would you like to have it in bed, or on the outside terrace?"

"The terrace will be fine."

Falisa stood up, stretched her arms high above her head. Dressed in a thin gown, she quickly wrapped herself up in a robe and tied it up. Falisa walked into the bathroom, where she brushed her teeth, washed her face, and carefully stared at her reflection in the mirror.

"Like I take threats lightly," she said to her reflection.

She stripped herself naked and turned on the water in the huge walk-in shower. She carefully stepped inside, and allowed the hot steaming water to massage her body.

Twenty minutes later, Falisa was dressed and sitting in her wheelchair outside on the terrace. The marble table was decorated with a linen cloth, and her nurse poured Falisa a hot, steaming cup of coffee. Omelets, hash browns, and a couple of well-done T-Bone steaks adorned the table. Falisa probably wouldn't eat more than the lean meat in one piece of steak.

Her nurse decorated her plate and placed it in front of her, and then she prepared her own plate and sat down. She looked across the table at Falisa, a fork in one hand and a steak knife in the other. "I barely got any rest last night," The nurse said while carefully dicing up her steak.

Falisa looked across the table at her nurse and noticed that she had on a light touch of make up this morning, as if she had somewhere to go. Keeping her thoughts and words to herself, Falisa kindly asked her. "Why couldn't you sleep?"

The nurse politely chewed on a small, square piece of steak. Her eyes met Falisa's eyes and she smiled. "Just thinking about your story," she said. "I'm still ready to hear the rest of it, if you don't mind."

Falisa's eyes went down to her omelet as she stuck her fork into it. She eased a small piece into her mouth and began chewing slowly. Her eyes lifted. She stared her nurse directly into her eyes. "Are you sure you're ready for this?"

The nurse smiled and flashed an even set of white teeth. The first part of Falisa's life story was so thrilling, that there was no way she could resist the rest of it. The fresh morning breeze came from the ocean, and the nurse shivered. She nodded her head at Falisa. "I'm definitely ready," she said, and sipped her coffee.

Falisa sipped from her coffee cup as well, then took another long, deep breath and said to the nurse, "Have you ever heard the saying that sometimes you're so smart, you're stupid?"

"Yes, I've heard it before."

Falisa turned her wheelchair around and scanned the beautiful manicured lawn and sparkling ocean water. The nurse stared at the back of Falisa's head, and Falisa began to speak. "All my business is personal," she said, as she turned to face the nurse. "But I must tell you this."

# 1

The great escape of Timothy "Timbo" Walker had devastated the entire state of Georgia, but the city of Augusta was definitely in an uproar. Falisa was under surveillance and investigated with keen eagle eyes. The federal government and the Georgia Bureau of Investigations had waited 48 hours after his disappearance to begin questioning her about his whereabouts. She surely wasn't going to tell them that she was the one who ordered a hit on her own husband, so she just played her part as the shocked and worried wife.

Falisa saw the headlines in the Augusta Chronicle with a huge photo of her late husband, Timbo, on the front page with a headline that read: DRUG KINGPIN PULLS A WHODINI. She read the article with interest, while drinking a cup of coffee in Columbia County jail. At nine o'clock sharp, two deputies escorted her down a long, tiled corridor. She inwardly laughed her heart out. *This ought to be interesting,* she said to herself.

When she entered the small four-corner room, there were already two well-dressed and clean-shaven white agents inside waiting for her. One of them was short and stocky with sharp blue eyes and a square chin. He extended his hand first. "Good morning, Mrs. Walker." he said soothingly, and with a casual nod of his head.

Falisa gave him her hand. She was shaking like a leaf from a tree. "Good morning." she responded. Her eyes stared into his, holding his rough-thick fingers.

The other agent extended his hand. Falisa took it and put on the same show, allowing him to feel her nervousness. "Good morning Mrs. Walker. I'm agent Kent from the GBI. We're here this morning to ask you a few questions concerning your husband, if you don't mind."

"No sir, I sure don't," She kept her facial expression tight, only allowing them to see fear in her eyes. No smiling whatsoever, unless there was a damn good reason for it.

Falisa pulled out the chair that was in front of her. She sat down, and both agents sat across from her. Agent Kent placed his briefcase on the wooden desk that separated them. She faked a cold chill and hugged herself.

Her eyes cut over to the small coffee machine in the right hand corner. She looked back at the agents. "If it's not too much of a bother, may I have a cup of coffee, please?"

Agent Kent eyed her. "Coffee?"

She nodded.

The other agent stood up, went over to the coffee machine, got her a cup of hot coffee, and brought it to her. He sat down and they began questioning her. "Tell us a little something about your husband?"

"I'm scared of him," she said nervously. "If I make a statement and he finds out..." She began to shake her head.

"Mrs. Walker, we know your husband is a dangerous man—"

"Damn right he is! For all I know, he's somewhere waiting to have me killed. If somebody can escape the federal government, anything is possible."

"Who says he got away?" the other agent asked.

Falisa sipped her steaming cup of coffee. Her eyes cut up at him and she asked, "Have you caught him yet?"

"Not yet Mrs. Walker, but you can rest assured that we will."

She dropped her head as if she'd been defeated. "Y'all don't understand. If I testify against Timothy, he'll find me, he'll find my kids."

"Listen Mrs. Walker, I can assure you that—"

"No deal, nothing in black and white. I will not live my life running and hiding. I know him like the back of my hand. He moves in mysterious ways," she said, her eyes turning moist.

The room fell silent; both agents stared at her for a brief moment. A tear rolled down her cheek. She knew that with Timbo and all the major key witnesses dead, the only thing they had against her was a simple tax evasion charge that she would plea out to. She needed the extra time to think things through. Her plan was sure to work, and she was willing to put her life on it.

When she stood up, she extended a nervous hand that trembled like an elderly person in an old folk's home. Agent Kent stood and shook her hand. Their eyes locked. "Thanks," she said.

She gave her hand to the other agent, bowed her head, and wiped the tears from her eyes with the back of her hand.

When she got back inside her living quarters, she went to her cell that she shared with an older Spanish lady who barely spoke any English. The lady was short and stout with a round face and alluring brown eyes. She was reading a fashion magazine printed in Spanish.

Falisa closed the door and climbed into the top bunk without saying a word. She lay on her back and stared at the ceiling, lost in her own thoughts.

*Three to four years, at the most. Timbo's bitch ass is dead, and the feds don't have the slightest idea that I'm the one who orchestrated the entire move. A major connect for Fly and his* crew would raise the family capital by ten thousand percent. *She closed her eyes and pretended that she was floating in the clouds. A smile appeared on her lips.*

"Maria." she whispered without opening her eyes.

Her cellmate turned around on the stool of the desk. She dropped the magazine and looked up at Falisa. "Si?"

"I need your connections in Miami. Please give me one opportunity. My family is loyal."

"My family is loyal also, Falisa. They operate differently from Americans."

"I understand," Falisa whispered back, but never opened her eyes.

The room fell silent again. Maria buried her face in the magazine and allowed nearly five minutes of silence to pass.

Maria turned back toward her. "I have three wonderful nephews in Chia." Her Spanish accent made Falisa tune her ears in.

"Chia, what is that?"

"A small village in the mountains, 16 miles north of Bogota, Colombia. You wanna know what our favorite phrase is."

Falisa turned on her side and stared Maria in her eyes. "Yes, let me hear it."

"We buy you or we kill you. Your choice."

Falisa's eyes gazed into Maria's. "I'll put my life on myself," she whispered.

Maria bowed her head slightly. "Well then, I'll help you grow your riches."

Falisa sat up, her legs dangled over the top bunk. She jumped down and sat on Maria's bed and looked her in her eyes. She grabbed Maria's hand, brought it up to her face, and kissed the back of it. "Thank you, Maria."

Now it was time for her to put her pieces of the puzzle together.

# 2

The following day, Fly got the call from Falisa. Marriott. He was alone in an executive suite at The Marriott, resting and thinking with the phone pressed against his face. "Why you don't want me to go, Mama? These people need to meet me, not Papa. Not Smurf."

"I want you to stay there with Amil, Fly." she said, then added, "Besides, these aren't just regular people we're dealing with. Stay in Georgia, send Smurf and Papa—"

Fly's temper got the best of him and he interrupted his mother in the middle of her conversation. "Haven't I proven myself enough?"

"That's not the issue at hand," she said calmly from the other end. "When you're on a team, Fly, everyone has a position to play. Your father made several mistakes, and we're not following his blueprint. I need you there. You have a bigger focus, right?"

Fly shook his head, frustrated. He knew his mission was Hawk up in New York, but since the new plan had come about, he was conflicted.

"Let me go to Miami. I'll handle business, Mama. Just trust me this one time."

There was a long silence from the other end. Fly held the phone to his face, waiting for a response.

"Okay," she finally said.

*Fly smiled.* Good decision.

"Listen carefully. You'll leave for Miami tonight. Somebody reliable will accompany you. Reliable." she repeated.

Fly held the phone, thinking Smurf all the way. "I understand," he said.

THE FOLLOWING EVENING, Fly and Smurf landed at Miami International on a Delta flight. They traveled light with a Louis Vuitton duffle bag filled with one hundred and fifty thousand dollars in cash and another bag with three days' worth of clothes for the each of them. Per Falisa's instructions, Fly was to go outside, pull his cell phone from his bag and wave it at the first limousine that he saw. Fly did it without hesitation. A black Lincoln limousine pulled from behind a row of waiting cars and taxicabs.

Fly looked at Smurf. "That gotta be the ride."

Smurf lifted the Louis Vuitton bag and wrapped the strap across his shoulder. When he stepped off the curb, Fly followed behind him with the other duffle bag and cell phone in his hand. At the rear passenger door of the limousine, a blond female chauffer waited and greeted them with a bright, pleasant smile. Smurf stopped, and out of respect, he stepped to the side and allowed Fly to enter first. Fly got in and Smurf got in behind him. The door closed.

Inside the limousine, a soft, elegant song played, and the words were in Spanish. Across from them, a light brown Colombian man in linen pants, sandals, and a wife beater watched them from behind a pair of expensive designer shades. He slowly bobbed his head to the music, never saying a word to either of them. The limousine moved out into traffic, muscling its way onto I-95. The Colombian continued to watch Fly and Smurf until Smurf broke the silence.

He threw his head back. "What up, bro?" His eyes fixed on the Colombian.

He still didn't part his thin lips.

The phone inside the limousine rang and the Colombian answered in Spanish. He listened to the voice on the other end. "Si, Auntie Maria." he finally said. Then he listened again. He removed his sunglasses and sat them on the seat next to him. "Si, Auntie Maria." His facial expression changed. "One moment." His deep Spanish accent sounded very intimidating.

He politely handed Fly the phone.

"Hello."

"You made it, I see."

"Yes ma'am, I'm here."

"Introduce yourself, stay on top of everything you stand for, and remember, your word is everything. I'll contact you every day to get an updated status."

"Okay, talk to you later." He handed the Colombian the phone and he hung it up.

Now his attitude had changed. He extended his hand out to Fly, and Fly shook it. "I'm Carlos, my friend."

"I'm Fly," he said, then pointed at Smurf. "This my best friend, Smurf, right here."

Carlos let go of Fly's hand and shook Smurf's hand. "Smurf," he said with a smile, revealing ivory white teeth with oval shaped diamonds on each of them across the front. Smurf stared at his teeth in amazement.

"Damn! How much you paid for your teeth?"

"A whole lot of money. You like?"

Smurf's eyebrows bunched together. "Hell yeah."

Carlos flipped his wrist to check the time on his watch. Through the tinted window, he watched the Miami skyline. No more than twenty minutes later, they were turning from Biscayne Boulevard. They made a left onto Port Boulevard and proceeded over the bridge until they got to the entrance of the Port of Miami. When the limousine got to the checkpoint booth, a security guard allowed them through without any problems.

From the rear of the limousine, Fly and Smurf gazed through the tinted window at several yachts and cruise ships. The limousine finally came to a halt. The panel window that separated the rear of the limo from the front rolled down. Fly and Smurf both turned their heads and looked at the sexy blonde, but her stare was directly on Carlos.

"Are you boarding now?" she asked him.

Carlos nodded, gave her a smile, and she rolled the partition back up and switched off the engine. Smurf looked at Carlos. "We getting on a boat?"

Carlos eased his shades back on his face. "Yacht my friend, far better than a boat."

The female driver opened the rear door and Carlos eased around and stepped out. He inhaled the fresh air coming from the ocean. Horns blared from ships, and seagulls were singing in his ears. When Smurf and Fly stepped out, the blonde closed the door and Carlos led them to the entrance of a private yacht.

They walked through a sea of people, up a flight of stairs, and across a small plank with metal hand railings. Carlos was greeted by a short guy dressed as a crew member for the luxury yacht. Fly and Smurf both stared around in amazement. They had never experienced or seen anything like this in their lives.

"Gentlemen, allow me to take your bags," the short guy said to Fly and Smurf.

Smurf looked at him, and then his eyes shifted to Carlos. Carlos bowed his head, giving him permission. They entered the yacht's interior through a pair of automatic sliding doors. The inside was laced with exotic woods, including handcrafted maple burl and eucalyptus. There were marble floors and thick carpet. Carlos led them down a hallway, bypassing a wine cellar and an exercise gym with a glass wall. Finally, they stopped in front of a shiny brass elevator. Carlos pressed a button and the doors opened.

"Man, I didn't know a yacht had elevators." Smurf said as they entered the elevator.

No one responded. The doors closed, and Carlos pressed a button that had the letters GA on it. They went to the next floor and the doors opened. When they stepped off the elevator, they saw beautiful women everywhere. Some were naked and some in string bikinis. A tanned Chinese girl stopped in front of them with a silver tray filled with custom cigars. Her hair hung down to her waist, her breasts were exposed, and she wore only a pair of black thongs and matching heels.

Carlos removed one of the cigars, Smurf followed by grabbing one, and Fly did the same. They continued to follow Carlos. Women were stopping him to kiss his hand and each of his cheeks. He stopped and said something in Spanish, and two young females appeared. They were no older than sixteen years of age; one was Cuban and the other was a Brazilian cutie.

Carlos pushed the door open into one of the guest cabins. It had wall-to-wall thick carpet. Two queen sized beds and an octagon shaped Jacuzzi sat in the middle of the floor facing a glass wall with a view of the ocean.

"You two stay here," he told Fly and Smurf. "Beautiful girls, champagne, cigars..." He waved his hands.

Fly and Smurf moved into the room and the young girls stayed with them. Carlos turned and left, closing the door behind him. The Cuban and Brazilian girls began to undress them both.

The young Brazilian girl led Fly to one of the beds. He lay

back and rested on his elbows. She went straight for his penis and slipped it in her mouth, working her tongue and lips like a professional. Fly looked down at her, and began toying with her rose-red nipples, as his toes curled. Fly closed his eyes as she took him deeper into her mouth.

With a half-smile, she winked at him as she pushed him closer to the edge with her skill. *Now this, I can get used to,* Fly thought to himself.

# 3

Carlos went up to the Sky Lounge, an open room that was beautifully decorated with soft Italian leather, and glass paneled walls that slide open to reveal a superb 180-degree view. He took a seat at a huge round table with two other well-dressed Colombians, who were both his brothers. Carlos was the youngest one, at twenty-four. To his right was Cortez, he was thirty-three and the oldest brother. To his left was Pepé, who was twenty-nine years old. The three brothers were from Bogota, but they moved back and forth from Miami to Chia, running their drugs and million-dollar sex slave industry.

Carlos fired up his cigar and sat in his comfortable high backed leather swivel chair.

"Auntie Maria's guests are in their cabin," he said in Spanish.

Cortez stared at him, his green eyes blazing. "Have you done a background check on them yet?"

Carlos shook his head. "They're very young, still teenagers. Not old enough to have a criminal record."

Pepé looked at Carlos with his marble gray eyes. His thick moustache covered his top lip. "Okay, on the strength of Auntie Maria," he paused, then he looked at the other two brothers. "We should try a small test run, nothing major."

"Five hundred keys." Cortez responded and looked at the other two.

They agreed. That was simple, five hundred kilos of cocaine to them, was like five grams to a street hustler in the United States. "Still, you should get their names, addresses and all information," he told Carlos.

He picked up a bell and rang it. Within seconds, a beautiful Cuban female appeared. She had slanted eyes, very exotic looking, and dressed in a two-piece string bikini. He spoke to her politely in Spanish. She smiled and bowed her head, and then she left as fast as she had come.

Back in the cabin, Fly and Smurf were being fed exotic fruits and relaxing in the Jacuzzi, both with smiles across their faces. The jets underneath the water massaged them to the point that they wanted to take a nap. A knock came from the door, then it opened. It was the exotic Cuban girl from upstairs. She came in with a smile, a note pad, and a pen. She went directly to the Jacuzzi and sat down on the edge.

Smurf's eyes traveled from her face down to her center, where the material of the thong was wedged between the split of her vagina. *Damn!* He said to himself.

She smiled shyly and closed her legs. Then, in her broken English, she said. "Give me name."

At first, Smurf looked confused; his eyes squinted for a second or two. Then he gave her all the information that she'd asked for. Next, she went to Fly and requested the same. Before she left, she hooked her finger on the corner of her thong and pulled it to the side, revealing a beautiful shaved vagina. She took Smurf's hand and made him insert two fingers inside of her. She clenched around his fingers, removed them and then sucked her own juices from his digits. Without another word, she got up and left their cabin.

The girl beside him grabbed his penis underneath the water and massaged it until it grew long and hard, then she sat on it and began riding slowly. Smurf grabbed her small waist and pushed his penis all the way up inside her.

Her eyes rolled to the back of her head. "Mmmm," she barely mumbled.

They were having in the time of their lives. Switching from female to female, an hour had passed and they were still going. Fly was on the bed pouring sweat, he had the young Brazilian girl's face buried in a pile of pillows while he stroked her roughly from the back.

She looked back at him, chewing on the corner of her bottom lip. "Dick so good," she said, even her English was sounding better now.

He pounded harder. Their skin slapped against each other, blending in with the other sex sounds that filled the room.

Suddenly, the door opened. Carlos yelled out something in Spanish, and both females jumped up, quickly grabbed their clothes, and exited the room. Cortez and Pepé came in next. Pepé was carrying an ax and walking with it upside down as if it was a cane.

"My friend," Cortez said and extended his hand out to Fly.

Fly looked up at him, a cold stare in his eyes. Fly shook his hand and Cortez' grip was so tight Fly couldn't snatch his hand away from him.

"Somethin' you wanna tell us, my friend?"

Fly shook his head, confused. He looked toward Smurf for a suggestion. He was dumbfounded as well. Fly scanned the room. He saw Carlos with his beady eyes staring angrily and then Pepé with the ax.

Cortez snatched Fly up from the bed, then he pushed him roughly to the floor. Smurf stood quickly, but was stopped in his tracks by a gold plated .45 that Carlos pressed against his temple.

"Si," Pepé said, then he stood over Fly's naked body with the heavy end of the ax sitting in the center of his chest.

"Man, what's up?" Smurf said from the other side of the room. His eyes fixed on Fly lying naked in the middle of the floor.

"My friend, you killed members of our Cartel." Pepé said, looking down at Fly.

Fly's eyes showed fear. Pepé raised the ax high above his head, and with all the power he had, he wedged it into Fly's leg. He screamed out in pain.

"Si," he said.

Blood splattered everywhere, but when he swung again, his leg nearly came off.

FALISA AND MARIA were sitting in their cell alone, talking about life. Maria had shared family secrets with Falisa, and Falisa shared some things with her as well. Both experienced different cultures, and Falisa now realized how the Colombians operated and their reasons for placing women in power. Maria went inside her pillow and removed her cell phone that her people had purchased for her. When she looked at it, she noticed that there were three missed calls.

She knew something was wrong. She called the number back and her nephew, Carlos, answered immediately. They went back and forth for nearly ten minutes in Spanish.

Maria looked at Falisa in pure disgust and shook her head. "Si." She put the phone down and looked at Falisa. "Bad news."

Falisa's eyebrows rose and her mouth parted. "What is it?"

Maria took Falisa's hand and rubbed it. "Your son name came back positive. They murdered other Colombians in Miami."

"No, it's a mistake. I can explain," Falisa roared and stood up. Her eyes stretched wide. "Please don't let them kill my sons." She referenced Fly and Smurf, she didn't want anything to happen to either of them.

Maria stared at Falisa. She saw the pain and sorrow in her eyes, but she knew that there was little chance of them staying alive.

"Please Maria, just tell them I'll give myself." she paused, just to make sure her words were chosen correctly. "I'll give my life in exchange for theirs."

Maria's eyes searched Falisa's to see if she was actually serious about what she was saying. With a questioning gaze, she saw sincerity in Falisa's eyes. Maria shook her head slowly and spoke back into the phone. The conversation was straight Spanish, and they went back and forth for nearly three minutes. "Si... Si" was all Maria kept repeating, then she looked up at Falisa and examined her face and body. "She's pretty," Maria said.

Carlos said something to her again. Maria nodded, then handed Falisa the phone. Falisa took it and put it to her face. "Hello."

"We hold your family in Bogota until you come, no matter how long. But when you free, and I get you in my custody, we let them go."

Falisa swallowed. "I understand."

"Are you fully aware that you'll never return to America?"

"Yes... Please sir, don't kill them."

The line clicked.

Falisa broke down in tears. Maria stood and wrapped her

arms around her shoulders. "They... weren't responsible." She cried out.

Maria simply stated, "You make good decision, Si." She patted her shoulder and they sat down and had a long talk.

# BOOK II

FORTY MONTHS LATER

*Chia, Colombia*

# 4

On the back of an old military style service truck, Falisa rode on a bumpy dirt road for the sixteen miles from Bogota to Chia. In the rear of the truck, she was handcuffed, with a thick rope tied around her waist. The rope was linked to six teenage girls who had been bought and traded off by family members from other countries. Falisa rocked from side to side on the uncomfortable ride, while looking around at the sad expressions the other girls wore on their faces.

Falisa didn't know their purpose, but she definitely knew hers. She stared at a young beautiful bleach blond haired girl with blue eyes. Falisa could tell that she was no more than fifteen years old. She was from France and couldn't speak a bit of English. When her eyes found Falisa staring at her, she looked as if she had lost her soul. Falisa took a mental note of this, realizing that young girls were strictly being sold, just like herself.

She felt the truck change gears and begin pulling up a hill. The smell of diesel gas was heavy in the air. Still rocking side to side at every bump in the road, Falisa stared around the truck, taking close looks and glances at the young girls that were from all walks of life. In the corner to her right, there was a pretty faced Arabian with smooth beautiful skin and long silken hair. She was shaking uncontrollably as if she was cold. Falisa's eyes squinted, and it felt as if her heart had tightened with a sharp pain racing underneath her ribcage. She knew she was sick from something.

The truck slowed down and everyone rocked forward, then quickly found their balance. Falisa's eyes and senses went to high alert. The truck was slowing down. She looked at the rear of the truck, and for a brief moment, she stopped breathing.

The truck came to a complete stop. Every female in the rear of the truck's eyes were now alert except for the Arabian girl in the corner. The thick plastic tarp that covered the rear opening was lifted to reveal two Colombian guards dressed in military uniforms and strapped with mini-machine guns. Falisa's eyes began to move rapidly and fiercely.

One of the guards climbed in the back of the truck. "Everybody alive?" he asked in a deep Spanish accent.

Looking around, he walked through the truck, kicking their legs and feet to make sure. When he got to the rear, he noticed the Arabian girl was shaking uncontrollably. He knelt down next to her and placed his two fingers on her wrist to check her pulse.

"She's very sick," Falisa said in the little Spanish that she knew.

The guard frowned and looked back at Falisa with cold eyes. He stood up fully, and walked back to her. He placed the tip of his gun directly on her throat. "Who told you to speak?" he growled, only inches away from her face.

Falisa allowed a look of fear to jump into her eyes. Her mind was sharp as a razor. Whatever she had to do to stay alive and to free her son and Smurf, she would do. When she didn't respond, the guard touched her breast roughly. She didn't stop him.

He smiled, slowly backed away, and climbed down out of the truck. The guard slapped the side of the truck, and it moved forward. The truck continued up a hill and veered off another dirt road that took them further into a jungle atmosphere where everything was moist and damp.

The truck came to another stop, and there were more guards this time. The engine was switched off and the smell of ether and diesel mixed together in the air. Falisa was the first one to hop down, and the connecting line of girls followed behind her. Standing in line at the rear of the truck, Falisa looked around in pure amazement. They were surrounded by trees, the majority of them were eucalyptus, and a host of Colombian guards.

One of the guards stared hard at Falisa. He walked up to her with a piece of paper and an attached photo of her in his hand. He examined her up and down, and pulled out a two-way walkie-talkie and said something into it. A voice came back from the other end. "Bring her to me."

The guard uncuffed her and removed the rope from her waist. She massaged her wrist, carefully running her fingers along the welts left from the cuffs.

Falisa rode on the passenger side of a topless jeep, a rough, hard-looking Colombian drove, and another one stood in the rear behind a 50-caliber machine gun with a string of bullets. After a short drive, they reached their destination.

The all-white mansion was three levels, surrounded by tall palm trees that were lined up parallel across the front. In the front of the mansion, two white stretch limousines sat in the circular driveway. They pulled behind the rear limousine and got out.

The guard on the rear escorted Falisa to the front door. With perfect timing, the double doors opened from inside and

Cortez stood there in linen pants, sandals, a wife beater, and a Desert Eagle sitting in a leather shoulder holster. His eyes scanned her up and down, then he looked at the guard and slightly bowed his head at him. He saluted Cortez, turned on his heels and walked away.

His eyes went back to Falisa, examining her facial features. Her face was oval shaped, and her eyes were sharp and intelligent. She was dressed in a two-piece army fatigue baggy suit. He stepped aside and allowed her to come in. Falisa walked in and stood in the marble foyer. Cortez closed the door and locked it.

He called out to someone in Spanish, and within seconds, a Colombian lady appeared, dressed in a maid uniform. "Take her. Clean her up."

Falisa looked at Cortez. "What about my son?"

Cortez walked off without responding.

"Hey!" Falisa yelled, hating to be ignored.

"Callate wey!" The maid hissed to Falisa.

She placed a finger on her lips and gave her a look as if to say that she should never yell in the presence of Cortez. The maid led Falisa toward the west wing and into a huge bedroom with huge gothic windows and four brass post canopy king sized beds. None of the beds was occupied. She led Falisa across the marble floor and into a bathroom with a huge walk-in shower that was surrounded with sheets of glass.

"Naked. Take shower." was all she said. Then she walked out and closed the door.

Falisa shook her head, hoping that they hadn't tricked her over here, and hadn't already killed her son and Smurf. She took her clothes off and her body odor rose into her own nose, which made her frown.

# 5

Deeper into the jungle, was another part of the compound that housed criminals. Those who stole cocaine, murdered and raped women, refused to work, and tried to escape the labor of manufacturing the cocoa plants to paste, and slave women who went against their boss's commands. Either way, everyone that was incarcerated and lived in the six-foot tall wooden boxes that was smaller than a walk-in closet, was waiting to be executed. Amongst the two hundred prisoners, Fly and Smurf were the only two that were about to be released.

Each box was engraved with only a number, names weren't necessary. Fly was sitting on a small metal cot with a thin mattress, massaging the nub of his amputated leg. It had been over three years since the yacht incident, and he'd become used to not having both of his legs. When the slot in the door came open, he frowned at the daylight and shielded his eyes with his hand. The guard looked in at him, and then he put a flash light in his face. "Get dressed." he told him.

Fly looked at the guard. "For what?" he yelled.

The guard didn't respond. He closed the slot, and the small box got dark again. From the outside, Fly could hear keys rattling at his door, then the bolt being removed. The door came open, and once again, Fly frowned at the daylight. He grabbed his prosthetic leg from the corner, stuffed his nub inside it, and strapped it on. Dressed in only a pair of cut off fatigue pants, he stood up and pulled on a tee shirt.

Fly was now sixteen years old, and his hair had grown past his shoulders. With a thick moustache and smelling like a dead animal, he stepped outside the box for the first time in nine months. He took a deep breath and looked up above and saw monkeys jumping from tree to tree.

When he gathered himself, and collected his thoughts, he yelled down toward the box where Smurf was. "Smurf."

"Callate wey." One of the guards yelled at him and pushed him forward.

The three of them walked in the direction of the box where Smurf was housed. They stopped, opened his slot and told him the same thing. "Get dressed."

When Smurf stepped out, he looked tired. His hair was long and bushy, and he had a full beard. He stood six feet even, and was now nineteen years old. He looked at Fly and didn't know if he should smile or cry. "Where we going?" he asked without any enthusiasm in his voice.

Fly couldn't tell him, but one thing they knew was that they weren't going before the firing squad, because they did that at night. A Colombian dude yelled out from one of the boxes. "Hey punta. Why you let the fuckin' Americans go?"

The guard ignored him, then they escorted Fly and Smurf to the waiting jeep. They jumped in and the driver took off.

It took them nearly twenty minutes to arrive at the all-white mansion. They parked behind the limousine and the guard from the rear escorted them to the front door. This time, Carlos appeared at the door. He looked at Fly and Smurf, his eyes wide from cocaine use. Holding a bottle of Jose Cuervo in his hand, he didn't recognize either of them. He looked at the guard and said something in Spanish to him, he responded back.

Carlos' eyes went back to them, then he examined Fly's leg, remembering the day from the yacht. He allowed them to come in, and he closed the door behind them. When Cortez appeared, he stared at Fly and Smurf for a short period of time. He then looked at Carlos and said something to him in Spanish. He escorted Fly and Smurf through the mansion where they would shower and dress in something more appropriate.

Cortez walked to the room where the maid and Falisa were. Falisa was sitting on a leather ottoman, wearing a colorful sundress. She slipped her feet into a pair of peach colored heels, and looked up at Cortez. Their eyes locked. He walked up to her and grabbed her hand. She stood up, and he slowly spun her around, examining her Coca Cola shaped body. He sniffed her neck, and his eyes began to glisten with excitement.

Cortez touched the ends of her shoulder length hair, his breath laced with alcohol. He faced Falisa and kissed her lips. Pulling her close to him, he palmed her ass cheeks and she felt him growing hard in his pants. Cortez unzipped his pants and sat down on the ottoman, then pulled out his thick, hard penis.

Falisa looked down at him. She was worried, but wouldn't allow it to show. "What about my sons?" she whispered.

"Si. No worry. We see them in a minute." he said, and pulled her dress up.

He made her sit down on his penis. She tried to slide down on it slow, but then he rammed it in her and she screamed.

ON THE OTHER side of the mansion, Fly and Smurf showered. A Colombian butler brought out a measuring tape and stood in front of Fly. He made him hold his arms out, then he measured his pants leg length. Thirty minutes later, they were both shaved and well-dressed in some old clothes that the drug lords wore last year. The butler brought them out and led them to a huge dining room to a colossal mahogany table that sat twenty people easily. However, the only people in the room were Cortez, Carlos, Pepé, Falisa and four armed and ugly goons.

Falisa stood up when she saw Fly, but Cortez ordered her to sit down, and told her not to say one word. That definitely puzzled her. She at least thought that she would be able to hug them. She covered her mouth with both hands, and her eyes teared up.

Fly and Smurf were ordered to take a seat across from her. Neither of them said a word, but they both stared at Falisa and were desperately wondering what she was doing there.

Cortez looked at Fly and Smurf with their hair long and naturally dreaded. "You two will leave Colombia today," he said. "Your mother gave herself up for the both of you."

Fly looked Falisa in her eyes and they stared at each other for what seemed like forever. He wanted to say something to her, but he knew for the sake of their lives, he couldn't.

She brought her finger up to her lips, and her eyes asked him a question; the same question he'd been asked by her for years. *When you look at me what do you see?*

Power. Strength. Queen.

When she moved her lips, he read them, and it was only two words.

The throne.

Fly studied his mother. Staring into her eyes told him so much. Her look gave him power and strength, as if a magnetic field drew them together. He took a deep breath.

Smurf stared at her long and hard. He still couldn't believe that this lady had the heart to give herself up, and be willing to stay all the way in South America with a family of drug lords. *She spared our lives, not them.* He smiled at her. He could see that she thought things out differently than most. He was willing to put his life on it, that she had a well laid out plan.

# 6

It was early December 1996 and cold. Fly walked through Hartsfield-Jackson International dressed in a black cashmere sweat suit. His limp was light, and barely noticeable. Smurf walked in stride next to him. Both of them were anxious, and definitely glad to be back home. When they stepped outside through the automatic doors, the cold North Georgia air greeted them with open arms. *Damn!* Fly said to himself and shivered.

They stopped briefly, scanned the congested airport traffic, then a horn blew from an all-white limousine. The rear door flew open, and Pig Man stepped out in a black waist-length mink coat, jeans and Alligator skin boots. He still looked the same, except he'd grown dreads. He walked up, and the three of them had one big group hug.

He pulled back smiling, looking from Fly to Smurf in pure amazement. "Yawl the baddest muthafuckas I know," he said and turned. "Let's go."

They followed Pig Man to the rear of the limousine. He stepped to the side and allowed them to enter first, then he got in and closed the door. It was dark and 2 Pac was bumping through the speakers. Pig Man pressed a button, and a row of pin lights illuminated the rear of the limousine. Pig Man unzipped his coat and shrugged out of it. He couldn't help but smile at them.

"Do yawl niggas know how powerful your presence is? Everybody thank yawl niggas dead." He pulled out a bottle of champagne.

Fly stared at him long and hard, not smiling at all. "I need to get to Augusta as soon as possible," he said. "I need to see my sister."

"We on the way now, lil brah."

"So update us." Smurf said coldly.

Pig Man popped the cork on the champagne bottle. He offered them some, but they both declined. He turned the bottle up. "We got some money, first and foremost. Should be close to two million. I don't count it, I just get it."

Smurf looked impressed at that, glad they didn't have to start from scratch. "I like that." he said, nodding his head. He leaned up and reached for the champagne bottle.

Pig Man handed it to him and his eyes went to Fly. "Amil has grown up. I don't have to tell you that she's fourteen now. Smart as hell, brah. Iris and Papa have been taking good care of her. She speaks Spanish real good." He paused and looked at Fly in excitement. "Listen brah, She the smartest fourteen year old in the CSRA (Central Savannah River Area). Iris has really brought her to life."

"That's good." Fly said. Then he asked him. "You know the situation with my mama right?"

He nodded. "I spoke with her every week for the last three years. I got the utmost respect for her. She did what any real queen would."

Silence hung in the air. Fly was lost in thought, mind moving in nine different directions. "You thank we can pay the

Colombians a couple million to get her back?" He asked Pig Man in hopes of a strong positive answer.

It didn't take Pig Man long to analyze the question. This was something that he'd been asking himself for the last three years. His eyes darted from Fly to Smurf, and back to him. "Anything is possible, that's why I've been saving. That was the first plan that came to Falisa. When she brought it to me, I cosigned it right away. We got an offshore bank account set up. Iris know them numbers and shit like that. I just handle the streets. But so far, we got like 1.2 million in separate accounts. Falisa was hoping we could have at least five million by time she was released, but we had a few bumps in the road and a few losses that led to us having to lay low for nearly a year."

Smurf sipped from the champagne bottle and looked at the Atlanta skyline through the tinted window. Without looking at Pig Man, he asked him, "What kind of bumps in the road?"

"Nothing major. A few niggas fucked up a few bonds. I'm talkin like a quarter million. Falisa had the final decision, though. We had to off four niggas in the process," he shrugged. "My name came up, even though Iris was the one put in the work. I had to take the heat. So I got a condo up here in Stone Mountain."

Fly and Smurf were soaking it all in, now they knew the plan. Get up five million and take the offer to the Colombians for his mother. Then Pig Man said, "You wanna hear some funny shit, though?" He looked at both of them.

Nobody responded, so he went on. "Timbo is number one on the America's Most Wanted list." he smiled. "Iris went down to number three, but she fluctuates up and down like the stock market."

They both cracked a smile and just shook their heads. "So you're not going down to Augusta?" Fly asked.

He shook his head. "I'll get dropped off. The driver will take yawl down there."

"And what about the New York niggas?"

"Since yawl been gone, Papa been up there three times. The first time he stayed six months, but he didn't have no luck. He paid a bounty hunter thirty thousand to find Timothy Walker Jr. One year later, we got a call saying that he was dead. Of course, Papa wanted to get it confirmed. So we went up to New York to a morgue in Harlem somewhere. Papa got the prints from the dead man, and guess what?"

"What?"

"It wasn't him. So, he still somewhere. We know what he looks like, though." He got the bottle back from Smurf and turned it up. "We still got a lot of work to do." He cut his eyes down at Fly's leg. "How ya' leg?"

"So-so," was all he said.

He stared out the window and thought quietly to himself as watching the illuminated skyline pass by.

# 7

It was over two hours later when they arrived at the farm that Papa Bear owned. The limousine crept through an uneven dirt road, deep in Harlem, Georgia. Smurf looked out the window, slightly buzzing from the champagne he'd drunk earlier. Looking up toward the sky, he noticed the bright full moon. When the limousine stopped, it was sudden. They jerked forward, the tinted partition that separated them from the driver rolled down. When they looked through the front window, they saw Papa Bear standing out front in an army fatigue jacket.

He walked to the driver side and told the driver, "You're on private property."

"Papa, it's us," Fly said.

Papa Bear looked toward them and squinted his eyes, not recognizing them through the long hair. "Wonderful. Yawl get out and we'll walk from here."

Fly and Smurf stepped out of the car onto the soft red dirt. Papa Bear greeted them both with a hug. The limousine backed out, and the three of them walked toward the ranch house. When they finally made it to the house, they went through the front door. The spacious living room was furnished with expensive suede furniture, and thick carpet stretched wall-to-wall. Papa Bear locked the door behind them. He flipped on the light and took a closer look at both of them. He was impressed.

They finally sat down, facing the blazing fireplace. Photos of Amil were in frames on the coffee table. Fly picked up the picture of Amil sitting on the floor next to the huge head pitbull. Her smile was beautiful.

He looked up at Papa Bear. "Where she at?"

"In the back, second room on the right."

Fly stood up and went toward the hallway, bypassing the first room and softly knocked on the door. When no one answered, he turned the knob and pushed the door open. He heard a light growl, then he heard her voice.

"Sit down Bo. Come here."

Fly swallowed. He had butterflies in his stomach, then he flipped on the light. Amil rose up in bed and rubbed her eyes to make sure she wasn't dreaming. She paused, her mouth opened in pure amazement.

"Fly?" she yelled and flipped the covers back. She ran toward him and hugged him. She held him tight.

He held onto her also, and she began crying on his shoulder. "It's alright," he told her.

"I know, I just miss you," she said, and pulled back from him. She examined him from head to toe.

He examined her as well. She stood five-six and was fourteen years old. She looked like a young Falisa with dimples, almond shaped eyes, and a mature body.

She looked down at his leg. "Is it true?"

"What?"

"That you lost your leg."

His head moved up and down.

"How?"

"I went swimming with the sharks," he said. He paused briefly, and then he added, "And I made it out alive."

"Interesting." she said and touched his hair. She turned up her nose a little. "This needs washing."

He smiled and moved his head back, then he looked down at the pit-bull. "See you still got Bo." He bent over and touched his head.

Bo playfully snuggled up against him. Amil looked at Bo, her eyes squinted and it was as if the dog recognized her stare. He slowly pulled away from Fly. She then smiled and displayed braces on her teeth. She took both of his hands in hers and pulled him over to the bed. She sat down Indian style and he sat next to her.

"I love to hear stories," she said. Her eyes had a hidden coldness. Then she asked him. "Why was I kidnapped?"

"Because of a mistake that I made."

Amil looked at him long and hard. His answer wasn't enough for her, but she decided to leave it at that for now. She quickly asked him another challenging question. "Are you going to kill them for it?"

That question caught him totally off guard, to the point that he frowned. "Why? Where all this come from?"

She smiled, and carefully placed a hand on his shoulder. "I'm only kidding, Fly. Where's your sense of humor?"

She seemed cunning to Fly. While he stared at her, he quickly remembered what Pig Man had just told him about her being incredibly smart.

Fly stood up. "You remember my friend Smurf, don't you?"

She rolled her eyes, and lay back on the bed, and pulled the covers. "I'm not interested," she said. "Cut the light out before you leave."

Fly stood there for a moment. He watched her, but she never looked back at him. He turned off the light and went back into the hallway. In the living room, Iris had appeared.

He smiled when he saw Iris. She stood up and they embraced. "Well, well, well," she said happily. "Glad you made it back."

"Glad to be back." he said to her.

They sat down next to each other on the sofa. Papa Bear was in his recliner, and Smurf was on the loveseat with his shoes off.

Smurf looked at Fly. "How Amil doing?"

Fly looked at him and shrugged. "I'm assuming she's alright."

Iris addressed the room. "Amil is wonderful and highly intelligent. She come and goes sometimes, and tends to get out there." Her eyes went around the room to everybody. "The doctors have ran tests on her, and she's a genius by far. You'll definitely be surprised."

Fly stared off in space, he had weight on his shoulders with his mother, and he was concerned about his sister. "We need to go to New York," he said.

Papa Bear turned his attention on Fly, staring at him without saying one word. He admired his heart and ambition. Still, he never said a word. They only heard the wood cracking from the fireplace.

Inside Amil's room, she was standing at the door with it thinly cracked. Her ears were tuned in to their conversation. *What are you waiting on, Papa?* She thought to herself, raising her eyebrows in question. *Respond damnit!*

"I knew you would be ready to continue that mission. That's why I went up there. We have an apartment to lay our heads, and we also have one for the mattresses."

Amil heard Papa Bear loud and clear. She squinted her eyes, thinking about the mattresses. What was the mattresses? *We have one for the mattresses.* She repeated it in her head again. She closed the door and quietly moved across the room, went to her desk, and turned on her computer. The light blue screen illuminated her bedroom.

She typed in: What is mattresses?

Something you sleep on.

She shook her head. Then typed again.

Definition of Mattresses? Nothing she was looking for was returned.

She stared at the computer screen, thinking hard. Papa used this term. She was thinking long and hard. Then she typed: Gangsters and Mattresses.

Mafia terms and meaning of going to the mattresses.

When she read it, she began to smile.

# 8

In Chia, Colombia, Falisa was on her twelfth day of residence at the all-white mansion. Inside the bedroom with the four canopy beds, she lay in a satin nightgown with a naked Cortez. Falisa fed him grapes and fresh exotic fruit as he lay on his back with his hands behind his head. Soft music played throughout the room, and Cortez was enjoying himself.

Falisa massaged his legs, beginning with his feet and working her way up one leg at a time. Cortez reached out and touched her firm breasts. Her nipples hardened instantly. She was trying to get used to being a sex slave, and would do whatever it took for her to stay afloat, and to stay out of the boxes in the jungle where two of the younger girls that came with her had already been sent with no chance of coming back alive. When she got to Cortez's thigh, she grabbed his penis, politely kissed the head, and quickly deep throated his six-inch shaft. Cortez smiled and closed his eyes.

She crawled up, straddled him and guided his penis into her tight vagina. She moved her body with a rhythm she heard in her head. Slow grinding, Cortez pulled her down and began sucking on her nipples; the left, and then the right one. When she squeezed the muscles in her vagina, making it grip tight around his penis she looked him dead in his eyes. She knew he was about to cum, he always did when she worked her body magic. After he came, he laid there for a minute.

She didn't get off, but she didn't care. When he got up, she went and took a steaming hot shower, thinking about her entire life as the water washed over her body. She scrubbed her mouth and tongue and washed between her legs. Then she said a silent prayer for herself.

After she showered, she slipped into a pair of clean panties and wrapped a towel around her body. When she went back inside the bedroom, the lights were dimmed. On her bed, Pepé now waited for her behind the white see through drapes. She stood there for a minute, hoping that he didn't think she was about to have sex with him. She didn't mind Cortez by himself, or even Carlos; at least he could fuck.

She stood there looking down at him. He looked at her and motioned for her to join him. *Now here comes the bullshit.* She thought to herself. She sat down on the bed. He reached and tried to remove her towel. She gripped it tight and gave him a confused look. "We can't." she said. "I belong to Cortez only."

Pepé's eyes turned cold, then he snatched her towel with force, bringing her entire body backwards. Pepé grabbed her around her throat, and pinned Falisa to the bed. Her air was cut short. He sat on top of her and noticed her eyes were turning red and watery. "You no belong to Cortez. You fuck whoever wanna fuck. Is that understood?" he growled.

She nodded her head to the best of her ability.

Pepé released his hold on her neck, and roughly snatched her panties off. She had a look of death in her eyes and he noticed it. "You angry, bitch?"

He gritted his teeth and squeezed his body between her legs, forcing her to spread them open.

Falisa changed her demeanor and allowed her body to relax, and within two seconds, her eyes were giving off a seductive stare. When Pepé pulled out his penis, it was soft. When he laid it on the lower half of her stomach, she felt how heavy it was. She looked down; he was big and thick. When their eyes met, he was smiling. Pepé was equipped with eleven inches.

"Si." he said.

Falisa grabbed him and massaged it until he began to grow. He took it from there and parted her pussy lips with his head. She eased further down to gain a better position. He eased down in her gently, dropping two inches in her at a time. She didn't expect him to show any tenderness. He was just angry and had nearly choked her to sleep, now he was displaying another side. She definitely made a mental note of that.

Falisa spread her legs further. Her eyes turned passionate, and her soft moans began to escape her mouth. Pepé's breathing sped up; she was tight. Her vaginal walls squeezed him firmly, her nails raked across his back, he dropped all he had inside of her. Just when he knew she was gonna scream like all the rest of the women he'd been with in the past, the response she gave him freaked him out.

"Si, Pepé. Si," Her nails clawed his back again. He picked up the pace of his rhythm, and leaned down and nibbled on her earlobe.

She was breathing on his neck, then she kissed him there, her tongue soft and wet. "Si, Pepé. Si" she whispered in a soft melody.

He was long stroking her now. She grabbed his face and made him kiss her lips. She said to him between kisses, "Si, sweet Georgia peach, Pepé."

Pepé looked her in her eyes. He noticed that she looked as if she was about to cry. He kissed her and pulled back. She grabbed his chubby waist and pulled him in. "Si, sweet Georgia peach, Pepé." she repeated again.

Pepé nodded, he was feeling himself about to come. He began driving harder and harder. "Si," he whispered. "Sweet Georgia peach, Pepé." He was so gone he called out his own name.

Falisa smiled as he came. He yelled out and fell on top of her. "My sweet Georgia peach," he whispered.

That's exactly what Falisa needed to hear. However, she didn't stop there, she grabbed him around his waist and grinded against him slowly, meeting his humble thrust. "Kiss me, Pepé," she whispered.

Pepé dove face first, his tongue twirling around hers. She mumbled. "Si, I need you to fuck me every night, Pepé." Her eyes stared into his.

Pepé couldn't believe the effect that Falisa had on him. Her sex was foreign to him. She worked her body in a professional rhythm. Her voice was seductive, and she was driving him crazy. Falisa squeezed his ass cheeks and pulled him into her. He tried grinding, but he'd gone soft. He gave her a look of embarrassment. He was proud of the size of his penis, but his performance and stamina wasn't up to par.

She kissed his lips. "It's okay," she whispered.

His eyes rolled to the top of his head. She grinded on his soft penis until she came. She squirted while rubbing her fingers through Pepé's hair. "Promise me you won't hurt me, Pepé."

He looked her square in her eyes, laid his hairy chest against her breast, allowing the tip of his nose to touch the tip of hers. "I promise, Si." He whispered. "Our secret."

# 9

Fly carried a chip on his shoulder against New York, even though neither the city nor the state had done anything to him. He'd made up in his mind that he would forever search for Hawk and his crew. It was now early in January of 1997, and snowing in New York. From the 45th floor of the Orion Condo, Fly stood next to Papa Bear in front of a nine-foot floor-to-ceiling window. Their view was cinematic. They could see the Hudson River and the George Washington Bridge. The city skyline was beautifully lit up.

Fly turned and went to the sofa and sat down next to Smurf where he was looking at some photos of Hawk. Fly studied his eyes. His stare was cold. He knew he was heartless, and didn't give a damn about anything.

Without turning and facing them, Papa Bear said, "New York is a big city, dangerous too," he began, "but on the average, a nigga from the streets don't expect retaliation after three years. So, there's no way possible that they're prepared for the unseen."

Fly looked at a photo of Hawk, but in his mind, he heard Amil's voice in his ears.

"So going to the mattresses means you're going to war?"

"Where did you hear that from?"

"Well, I kind of overheard you and Papa talking. And I thought I'd share something with you."

"I'm listening."

"One of them has three fingers missing on his left hand, and I think his name is Oz."

Fly had her words tattooed in his memory. He knew they had a name and face for Hawk, and they had a brief description on Oz, whose name was actually Ox. They were close like a hide-N-seek game.

He slowly looked up at Papa Bear, and in a calm and easy voice, he asked, "So what's the next move we make?"

Papa Bear stood firm and strong. His massive arms clasped behind his back, still staring out the nine-foot wall of glass overlooking the illuminated New York skyline. With more plays than an NFL quarterback, the first play was bringing eight additional men with him that he knew from several years ago. They were certified killers from Georgia and the swamps of South Carolina.

He'd purchased four apartments over a year ago, and had also bought four used yellow taxicabs. Papa Bear ordered them to travel in pairs. One man would drive, and the other one would be disguised as a passenger. They rode around Queens, Brooklyn, Bronx and Harlem with a photo of Hawk taped on the thick bullet proof glass with bold letters just below it. WANTED: $100,000 REWARD. Under that was a 1-800-phone number that went straight to Papa Bear's cell phone.

For the last four days, his men had been touring New York in hopes of a stranger getting into the back seat and recognizing Hawk's face. He knew that in due time, someone would call. Meanwhile, Pig Man rode the subways in New York pretending to be a bum, checking for any leads on anybody that went by the name Ox.

Papa Bear didn't want Fly and Smurf to hit the streets alone, even though they both were ready, certified, and highly anxious.

Smurf stood up, walked across the room, and stood next to Papa. "So, if we're not gonna get no action, why did we come?" he asked him.

"So ya'll can watch my back." He put a hand on Smurf's shoulder. "We will not leave New York until we get our guy, or we get us enough money for Falisa."

Fly looked up at him, then a smile appeared.

"Now ya'll get some rest," he said. "We got an entire month ahead of us."

ONE WEEK LATER, Papa Bear got a call from one of his hired henchmen. He listened to the conversation intently, hung up and got Fly and Smurf. They rode the elevator down to the lobby. Papa Bear dressed in a suit and tie, and Smurf and Fly were dressed like your typical New Yorker. Baggy jeans, Timberland boots and Goose feather jackets. The wind sliced through their clothes as they stepped out onto 42nd street.

A yellow taxicab crept up next to them. Papa Bear noticed his associate driving. He got in the front seat, and Fly and Smurf bounced in the backseat. For the next hour, they rode through the crowded streets of New York until they arrived at their destination, a small warehouse building that they'd rented across town. The driver blew the horn, and the garage door opened. They pulled inside and the door closed down. The warehouse was cold and dimly lit. All four cabs were parked next to each other in a line. When they stepped out the cab, they noticed a long wooden fold out table that was equipped with a forty-inch TV, a VCR, and four Bose speakers that would give them some quality sound.

Fly looked around. He was confused, and wasn't familiar with any of this. A short stocky guy in his late forties walked up and shook Papa Bear's hand, then Fly, and then Smurf, in that order.

"Glad you gentlemen could make it out." he said, then turned toward the TV with the remote in his hand. He pressed play, and the video of Amil came on. The only part shown was Ox was saying, "Seriously, This is not a Spike Lee joint."

The short man turned up the volume. He looked back at Fly. "Train your ears to his voice, only."

For the next fifteen minutes, they listened to the sentence over thirty times. Slow. Fast. Slow. Fast.

They brought in a guy in a tee shirt, jeans, and socks. His face was covered with duct tape, except his nose and mouth. The two goons that escorted him in, had his hands bound with plastic cuffs, and he was missing three fingers from his left hand. They brought the bound man up to the table opposite Fly, Smurf, and Papa. They clipped a mini microphone to the neck of his tee shirt.

"Okay, speak." The goon on the right side told him.

"Seriously, this is not a Spike Lee joint." he said, loud and clear. His voice boomed through the speakers, giving off a surround sound effect.

"Come again."

The guy repeated it.

"Come again."

Again, he repeated his sentence.

Everyone shook their heads. The two goons escorted him away, and within minutes, they came back with another guy. His faced was duct taped the same way, everywhere except for his nose and mouth. This guy was muscular with wide shoulders and had arms like Ray Lewis. He was missing fingers also, except his were missing from his right hand. They walked him up to the table, and quietly clamped the microphone to the collar of his shirt.

"Okay, speak."

"Seriously, this is not a Spike Lee joint." his voice sounded far too deep and scratchy.

"Come again."

He said it again.

The short man looked at Fly and Smurf. They waved him off. The goons removed the microphone and quickly whisked him away, and in less than two minutes, they were back with another guy that fit the missing fingers description. They brought him in, blood pouring from his face; he'd been badly beaten and was covered in tattoos from his neck down to his waist. The big guy was aggressive, and angry as a son of a bitch.

When they got him to the front of the table, he stood up. "I ain't sayin' shit." his voice boomed.

Papa Bear's cell phone rang. He answered it while walking toward the nearest cab. He got in the front seat. "Yes, Most Wanted Hotline."

"Hello." a female voice said from the other end. "Are y'all still giving out the reward for the guy, Hawk?"

"Yes ma'am, we're sure are." Papa Bear turned and snapped his fingers.

"Okay listen," the lady said from the other end. "I don't know where he's at, but can I like get some money for one of his associate's whereabouts?"

"If the information is reliable."

"Oh, it's definitely reliable. Listen."

## 10

It took an additional three days for Papa to organize his move. His law-abiding citizen had provided him with a positive ID of Hawk's right hand man, Cory. Word was that Cory had separated from Hawk after they'd robbed and killed the Colombians. He felt that Hawk had chumped him off by only giving him one hundred and seventy-five thousand dollars. He took his money and invested it into a brick of heroin, assembled his own team, and set up shop in Baltimore and New Jersey. In less than a year, he was worth a million, easy. He only showed his face in Brooklyn every other month, to stop by, scream at a few of his comrades, and show off his Maserati. Then he was ghost again.

Tonight, he was back in New York City at one of the most expensive restaurants in the world, called the Masa, where the fish was flown in straight from Japan. He sat at a table with a female model who had appeared in one of Jay-Z's videos. Cory wiped his mouth and left ten one hundred dollar bills on the table for him and his date. She flashed him a beautiful smile when he blew her a kiss.

"You ready, ma?"

She nodded.

Cory stood up, dressed in a special ordered Versace cashmere sweat suit. A platinum and diamond chain hung from his neck. The female stood up also. She was in fitted jeans, boots, and a waist-length leather jacket by Gucci with a matching handbag. They moved through the restaurant and headed out the front door where his Maserati was being brought up to him by valet. The Japanese driver stepped out and left Cory's Maserati running with the hazard lights flashing.

The model walked around to the passenger side and looked at Cory across the top of the car. Suddenly, four yellow cabs pulled up out of nowhere. Two masked men jumped out, guns drawn. Cory saw them coming, and had already pulled out a Glock .40. Eyes squinted, he aimed and squeezed the trigger. His Glock roared, discharging bullets in the direction of the two armed men. They ducked and returned fire. Corey couldn't get inside his car, bullets were whizzing past him.

Two more armed and masked men approached and closed him in. They rattled him with bullets until he slid down the car, leaving a trail of his blood. His foot was twitching, and screams and shouts filled the air. One by one, the taxicabs pulled off into the night.

When Papa Bear got the news, he couldn't do anything but shake his head in disgust. He dropped his phone on the couch and looked at Fly and Smurf. "They almost had him."

"What happened?" Smurf asked.

Papa Bear smiled. "He lived and died by the gun."

"So what now?" Fly asked in a disgusted tone of voice.

Papa Bear walked back over toward the window. "We wait patiently."

~

In the course of three weeks, things had changed drastically for Falisa. She was no longer a sex slave, due to the fact that Pepé had proposed to her and told Carlos and Cortez that he'd fallen in love with her. The brothers were totally against him marrying an American for one, and for two, they knew if she could seduce their brother Pepé, that she was capable of doing anything.

That morning, Falisa and Pepé sat outside on an open-air balcony in the east wing of the white mansion. The two were dressed and sitting at a round table eating fruit and drinking tea. The Colombians weren't big on breakfast and dinner, but lunch was like a ritual. Falisa looked up at him and flashed a gorgeous smile.

Pepé's eyes glistened with excitement. He loved her eyes and her smooth brown skin. When he got up, he kissed her lips passionately, nearly taking her breath away.

Her eyes closed. "Si, Pepé." she whispered.

He could feel her heart racing forward every time she made that statement. He took Falisa on a walk through the mountain trails where they had several huge Hippos playing in a lake of water. They held hands and listened to the wild life that surrounded them. They walked and talked. He shared his life with her, and she felt sorry for some of the things that he had gone through as a child. In return, she told him about her family and gave him details about what happened with her husband and the Colombians back in Miami.

Pepé stopped and pulled her close. Standing in the center of a manicured garden, he held her around her waist and kissed her neck. She closed her eyes, and his hands traced the curves of her body. She relaxed in his arms.

"You should marry me," he whispered.

Falisa wrapped her arms around his neck. "I will," she said. "But I must go back to the United States."

“Si, I got a mansion just for you in Miami. No one there.”

“Are you coming with me?” she asked.

“Can I trust you, Falisa?”

Falisa’s eyes teared up. Pepé’s heart tightened and he wiped her tears with his thumb. There wasn’t another word spoken.

## 11

It took nearly another month for Falisa to get everything ready and prepared. Pepé had taught her so much, and had literally fallen head over heels in love with her. They had a private wedding in Chia, and each of them wore a diamond and emerald wedding ring. Today, she was on a private jet flying over Miami, Florida. They bypassed Miami International. Pepé and his brothers had their own private airstrip where she was going to land.

She sat in a leather recliner sipping champagne from a glass, and occasionally glancing out the window at the dazzling Miami lights below. She was thinking harder than ever before. She wouldn't contact her kids until she was settled in and secure.

Falisa finally smiled and held out her hand. "My Ray Charles diamond," she whispered.

When the jet landed, she stared out the window at the darkness until it came to a complete halt inside a huge hanger. Falisa was escorted off the plane and straight into a stretch limousine. No more than thirty minutes later, the limousine was pulling into the driveway of an all-white mansion identical to the one in Chia. Tall palm trees lined the driveway.

The closer the limousine got to the front of the mansion, the harder her heart began to thump inside her chest. The lights were out in the mansion. The driver got out and opened the door for her. Falisa extended her hand. The stocky Colombian man took it, and she stepped out in expensive Louboutin heels and a dress that Pepé had bought for her.

"Gracias." she said with a smile. He bowed, then he produced a set of keys and handed them to her. Again, she said, "Gracias."

She turned and headed toward the front door of the mansion while the driver removed several pieces of luggage and foot trunks emblazoned with the LV logo. Pepé had taken Falisa to Paris to shop. They had also flown to Japan for one day, just for lunch, and Argentina to watch a polo game. He spoiled her outrageously.

When she entered the mansion, she deactivated the alarm while the driver brought in her belongings. Standing inside the marble foyer, the first thing she did was remove her heels and left them there.

She moved into the living room where everything was white marble, brass and wood. A huge Picasso hung from the wall over the fireplace. The ceilings were high, and an elevator was surrounded by two flights of half circled stairs. Falisa was impressed. She stood in the middle of the floor and looked up at the huge beautiful crystal chandelier that hung from the ceiling. She walked around the double stuffed suede couch, allowing her fingertips to trace across the material. Every piece of furniture was pure white, and she was definitely feeling the atmosphere. It gave her a surge of energy and an aura of power.

When she found the master bedroom on the third level, it was so beautiful and breathtaking that she nearly had an orgasm. She covered her mouth, enthralled by the beautiful view of the ocean from the balcony. When she opened the doors, the ocean breeze ruffled her hair and her dress. She stood there staring out into the ocean, lost in a long thought about how her life had been on the line, and how she'd turned everything around in her favor. Falisa was serious, educated, and dangerous.

She felt yet another surge of adrenaline run through her veins, and with pure energy and excitement, she yelled out to the top of her lungs. "I RUN THIS SHIT."

She paused, turned, and walked back inside the bedroom, which was decorated with Louis XVI furniture that was fit for a queen. She laid back on the comfortable king size bed and thought to herself. *The throne is mine.*

An old episode of Martin was playing on the TV where Sheneneh had sued Tommy for a little fender bender. They were in the courtroom and Tommy was doing a cross-examination.

"Sheneneh, you say you're a Christian woman... Yet you sit here and lie to these people." He gave Sheneneh an angry look while she sat on the stand with crutches and a six-inch foam neck brace.

"Now you better tell 'em the truth and tell it now."

Sheneneh looked around the courtroom. "Oh my goodness! Somebody get me in the witness protection program!"

Smurf and Fly erupted with laughter. Martin was a popular sitcom in its final season that had kept the world laughing for five years. Thanks to syndication, Fly and Smurf were able to watch the episodes that they had missed while locked away in South America.

Across the table in front of them, there was nearly three hundred thousand dollars lined, stacked and rubber banded. The money had come from Pig Man. It was from a robbery he'd pulled off on a couple out on Long Island. They still hadn't found Hawk or caught the right dude that went by the name, Ox.

Tonight, Papa Bear had yet another plan. He'd purchased some top of the line surveillance equipment that he hadn't used. They'd been in New York over a month, and still hadn't gotten their guy. He was beginning to feel agitated.

His cell phone rang. The hotline was back in motion. "Most Wanted Hotline," he answered.

"Papa." The female voice came from the other end.

His forehead wrinkled slightly, allowing the voice to register. He knew it was Iris, but he wouldn't mention her name over the phone.

"I'm listening," was all he said.

"It's time to come home," she said. "We got bigger plans now."

"And what is it? We're on to something big right now."

"Listen, the queen is here. She wants everybody to meet her."

Now Papa paused, spinning the statement around in his head. *The queen is here.* She couldn't be talking about Falisa. Or could she? Then he asked, "She's there at the farm?"

"No, in Miami. She'll be here tomorrow, and she's asking for everybody to be here."

Papa Bear gave a smile and stared at Fly and Smurf. Pig Man was coming out the kitchen with plates full of fried jumbo shrimps.

"We'll be on the first flight." He hung up, and then he addressed the room. "Excellent news," he said.

Their eyes went to him in question. "We found him?" Fly asked.

Papa Bear shook his head.
Everybody waited eagerly for the news.
"They've released Falisa." He told them with a rare smile.

## 12

The following evening, Falisa flew over the city of Augusta in the same private Learjet that had brought her to the United States a few days ago. From the window, she could see the beautiful green sea of grass at the Augusta National Golf Club below her. Falisa was a graduate of Paine College and grew up in Augusta. When she was younger, their middle school went on a field trip to the see the Masters golf course at the Augusta Club. She remembered the dark green grass, the beautiful shrubs, and the manicured garden. She closed her eyes, took a deep breath, and smelled the fresh air that lingered in the back of her mind so many years ago. Now that she was in position, she was definitely thinking strongly about going to see Tiger Woods play one day.

The Learjet landed at Daniel Field, located at Wrightboro road and Highland Avenue. The sun was setting and the sky had turned a burnt orange color. When the wheels touched the asphalt and began cruising, she was already on her feet. Dressed in a peach waist-length leather jacket that Pepé had commissioned Ralph Lauren himself to specially design for her, she wore fitting denim jeans and peach Polo riding boots.

When she stepped off the plane, she only carried a cell phone with her. At the bottom of the steps, she flashed a beautiful smile when she saw Fly and Amil standing next to each other. The three of them shared a group hug. Falisa teared up instantly as she held Fly in her right arm and Amil on her left. She pulled back and looked at her beautiful daughter and handsome son. She cried even harder. Amil cried with her and they held on to each other.

Papa Bear had a heart of steel, but as he watched the emotion filled moment, even he felt himself about to cry. Just thinking about what the three of them had gone through over the last couple of years was something that was entirely unheard of. Pig Man was standing next to him experiencing the same emotional effect. In the last four years, they'd become a tight secret family.

Falisa walked over to Papa and they hugged. "Thank you so much," she said in a cheerful voice.

"You're welcome."

She went to Pig Man and gave him the same emotional hug. "Thank you too."

When she let him go, she looked inside the Yukon that they'd arrived in. It was empty.

She looked at Papa Bear and everyone else. "Where is Iris?" Her eyes stopped on Amil.

She couldn't answer. When Falisa turned and looked at Smurf coming from the side of the hanger, she thought Iris would be coming behind him. Smurf smiled at Falisa and they embraced. She thanked him too, and when nobody responded about Iris, she knew that they had left her behind.

Falisa walked over to Papa Bear and casually pulled him off. They walked about eight feet next to each other in stride.

"What's the deal with Iris?" Falisa asked him, the winter air cut through her jacket. She then thought about everybody standing in the cold.

"She tells me that she is alright. She don't wanna chance it out in public."

Falisa's face saddened and she felt warm about it. "But she is okay?"

Papa Bear nodded.

Falisa smiled again and looked at everyone. "Y'all ready?" She moved toward the bottom of the steps and grabbed Amil's hand as she went.

Her and Amil boarded the Learjet first. Fly and Smurf went next, and Pig Man, then Papa Bear. When everyone found a seat, a personal attendant dressed in Khaki pants and a white shirt brought out drinks and a platter of diced fruit.

Smurf saw a remote and grabbed it. "What's up! See if Martin on."

Falisa sat on a loveseat and brought Amil in next to her. She held her strong face between her hands and locked eyes with her fourteen year old daughter. Then she kissed her forehead. "I love you sweetie," she whispered. "And don't never forget it."

"I love you too Mother." Amil spoke proper English, sounding a tad bit too prissy.They hugged again.

The attendant announced, "We're departing in ten minutes."

The plane was quiet. Falisa looked over at Fly. Even though he'd made a few bad decisions, she loved him dearly, and now she was ready to put him in position for the family throne. She knew that all he needed was the proper guidance, and he'd be in power for the rest of his life.

She scanned the rest of the faces that were closest to her. She thought about the absence of Iris, and everything that she had done for Falisa by being there every day, and every night for her daughter. Iris had been there to do the things that she couldn't do.

Suddenly, she looked at Papa Bear. "I wanna go to the farm. I need to see Iris."

Papa Bear looked at his watch. It was a little after six pm and it was dark outside. He stared at her for a brief moment, her eyes laser beaming into his. "Just you and I."

She looked around. "I'm sure everybody will be alright until we get back."

FALISA RODE on the passenger side of the Yukon while Papa Bear drove through the uneven dirt road. The headlights danced across the tress. "Real spooky out here," Falisa said, while looking out the window into the darkness.

"Only at night." Papa Bear responded as he turned down another dirt road.

While looking out into the darkness, she said, "If I'm not asking too much, I would like to see him."

Papa Bear's eyebrows bunched together. He looked at her, then put his eyes back on the road. "Who?" he asked, his voice steady and calm.

"Timbo." she responded.

"You want me to dig him up?"

"Is it a problem?"

He shook his head. "Not at all.

# 13

Inside the house, Iris was sitting next to the fireplace on the floor. She had a leather photo album in her lap with the pit-bull, Bo, lying on the floor next to her. Looking at the photos of Amil from the last couple of years was making her sad. Even though Iris was on the run, and probably still one of Americas Most Wanted fugitives, she was still living.

She had definitely become tired of running, and not being able to go anywhere was driving her crazy. When Bo stood up and his tail rose stiff in the air, she dropped the photo album, grabbed the mini assault rifle next to her, and went toward the front window. She pushed her back against the wall, and with a quick pull back of the action, she chambered the assault rifle and slowly parted the curtain.

She saw the headlights of the Yukon and wondered why they were coming back. When Falisa and Papa Bear stepped down from the SUV and closed the doors, Iris smiled and went to unlock the door. When she opened the door, Papa Bear stepped to the side and allowed Falisa to enter first.

Falisa stopped at the threshold and looked at the lady that stood before her. "Iris?" she asked and broke into a smile.

Iris nodded and smiled also. They hugged each other tightly like long lost sisters. This was their first time ever meeting face to face, yet they felt a deep electrifying power surge run through their bodies. Falisa cried, and so did Iris. When they got inside, Papa Bear closed the door, then disappeared into the back of the house.

Falisa and Iris found a seat in the living room. Bo stood next to Iris and looked at Falisa. She wiped tears away and looked Iris straight in her eyes. “How long have you been on the run?”

“Fifty-three months, all together.”

“And how long have you been here on the farm?”

“Maybe forty two months, I wanna say.”

Falisa touched her hair and brushed it from her eyes. “So, you just gonna stay here and do nothing?”

Iris looked deep into Falisa eyes, a strong and confident stare. “There is nothing else I can do.” Iris sounded defeated and tired.

“Come to Miami with me. I owe you that much, let me help you.”

“I don’t wanna take the risk of going through an airport, and I’m definitely not going in a car.”

Falisa took a deep breath. She couldn’t remove her stare away from Iris. A stranger that raised her daughter on the strength of being down right loyal. “I trusted you with my daughter’s life, and now I ask you to trust me with yours.” Falisa’s voice was low and strong.

Thirty minutes later, Iris had her bags packed. She loaded them into the rear of the Yukon. Bo stood next to her, wagging his tail and looking up at her.

Falisa looked down at Bo. Then she looked at Iris. “We’re taking Bo with us.”

“Wonderful, Amil will love that.”

They walked together. Iris popped on a flashlight and they walked around the back of the house. Bo led the way up the path that led them through a maze of trees. The night winter air was cold. They were both in jeans and jackets. They walked nearly a quarter of a mile through the woods until they found Papa Bear standing next to a pile of dirt where Timbo's body was buried.

Falisa and Iris walked up and stood next to him. He aimed his flashlight down into the six-foot deep hole. Falisa got the flashlight from Iris and aimed it at his skeleton bones and the burned tuxedo that he wore the day of his parent's funeral. She coughed up a hunk of spit, and out of anger she fired it from her mouth and directly into the skull of the corpse.

She stared at him for nearly five minutes, wondering why he turned on his family. Her eyes turned teary all over again.

"Do you know you caused your son to lose his leg?" her voice was low and calm. "You kidnapped my muthafuckin' daughter for your own good." She spit down at him again. Her anger was written across her face. "I gave myself up to become a fuckin' sex slave to get everything back on track, you no good son of a bitch. If I could bring you back alive, I would. Then I'd kill you again."

She took a long deep breath and got herself under control. She looked up at Papa Bear and silently nodded that she was finished and Timbo could be covered back up.

They returned to Daniel Field airport four hours after they had left, and they got straight on the private jet. Everyone was glad to see Iris and Bo. They strapped in and headed to Miami.

# 14

Hawk wasn't hiding from anyone. He was just a man who knew how to move. With penthouses in New York, Arizona, and now one in Atlanta, Hawk was a made man; young and rich. He'd built a music recording studio in Manhattan and produced an R&B group that was getting playing time on the radio stations from New York down to South Beach. He was rumored to be plugged in with a new underworld group of other street millionaires that operated under one accord: Secrecy.

He stood at the wet bar with a young beautiful female, both of them wrapped in silk robes. He poured two glasses of champagne, and served one to his companion.

The phone rang. "Peace," he answered as he tasted the expensive champagne.

"Yo, what's good, fam?" the voice said from the other end.

Hawk recognized the voice. "Yo. Who this? My nigga Rolex?"

"All day. Hi you, kid?"

"Damn! I'm blessed, son. You been missing, hi you doing?"

"Wonderful. I'm in Winston-Salem, got two kids and shit. Married, running my own business, I can't complain."

Hawk smiled and walked away from the bar. He went toward a suede couch in the living room. When he sat down, he sipped from his glass again and sat it on the table.

"Enjoying life, basically," Hawk responded.

"That's the bottom line, kid. Enjoying life," he said. "Did you hear about Cory?"

Hawk's eyebrows eased in together and his forehead wrinkled up. "Nah, what happened?"

"Word on the street is that he got hit up, but nobody know nothing. Brooklyn niggas saying it was Harlem niggas."

Hawk's face turned long and sad. Cory was still like a brother to him. They grew up together, wore the same size shoes, and spent the night over each other's houses when they were young. Despite the minor fall out they had after the lick, he still had love for him. Hawk rubbed his hand across his face and took a deep breath. "Man, I need to call his mother and send my condolences."

"Wow, you haven't heard for real, huh?" Lex paused on the other end. "They found his mother floating in the river."

Hawk dropped the phone and stared wide-eyed. He knew who it was; he could feel it. It was time to prepare.

AT THE ALL-WHITE mansion in Miami, Falisa arranged a formal dinner for her family. Servants brought out platters of fresh fish and an array of shrimp with rice and steamed vegetables. They all sat outside on the patio overlooking the ocean. Even though it was February, the South Beach weather was nice and warm. Falisa sat at the head of the gothic marble table. Fly was on her left, and Amil was to the right of her. Amil watched her mother's smooth and elegant demeanor.

Falisa held up her champagne glass. "This is to our success as a whole," she said.

Everyone around the table held up their champagne. Even Amil was allowed to have her very own first taste. Falisa clinked her glass against Fly's glass first, and he continued the toasting train around the table. When it got to Amil, she held her glass out to her mother, and Falisa smiled at her. Their glasses clinked together.

"For the next week, we'll all stay here together. I want each of you to know me, and I want to know each and every one of you. After that, we'll move forward."

Later that night, Falisa and Fly walked out into the maze garden in the rear of the mansion and found a seat on a concrete bench. The ocean breeze brushed across their faces and the atmosphere was wonderful.

The first question that Fly asked during their one on one conversation was, "What happened, and do you have to go back?"

Falisa wore a summer dress that evening, and she sat with her legs crossed. She looked her son straight in his eyes and said, "First of all, that could've been avoided. My gut feeling made the correct decision, and your heart took over good judgment. As of today, my decision will be the final one under any circumstance. Is that understood?"

Fly's eyes were on hers. "Yes ma'am."

She grabbed his hand and held it. "Now listen at me real good. I had to sacrifice myself for you and Smurf, and even more for my life. In doing that, I married Pepé."

Fly's eyes twinkled a little and then he squinted. He never removed his eyes from her. Staring blankly, he nodded without saying a word. His mind recalled the image of Pepé standing over him with his ax. He could still feel the pain from when he first chopped into his leg.

He squinted again, and his eyes narrowed. "I guess some things happen in life for a reason."

"Are you ready, Fly?" she asked him.

He nodded. "I stay ready."

She rubbed his hand. "Yesterday was the past, our test is ahead of us."

"So what about this nigga, Hawk?"

She patted his head. "In due time, baby," she said. "Trust my words, okay."

A few minutes after Fly left the garden; Smurf came and spoke with her. They talked for nearly twenty minutes, then Pig Man and Papa Bear came together. They both shared everything about how they met her son and Smurf. She was impressed. When they left, Amil and Iris walked out together. They sat down and Amil touched the ends of Falisa's hair.

Falisa looked at Iris and smiled. "I'll never be able to repay you."

"You already have. I'm just glad to be accepted."

Amil looked at Iris. She adored her for sure, and she had definitely become attached to her. "Iris is like you, Mother." Amil sounded polite and sincere.

"I'm sure," Falisa said. Her eyes went to Amil and she drew her closer, holding her daughter like a lovable Teddy Bear. When her eyes went back to Iris, she simply said, "The surgeon is flying in from Brazil tomorrow. Are you ready for a new life?"

Iris' heart fell into her stomach. At first she didn't know what Falisa was talking about, then it registered quickly. She was talking about paying for to have reconstructive surgery.

Falisa squeezed her shoulder. "I'll be with you every step of the way."

Iris smiled, and her eyes turned moist. She hugged Falisa and Amil at the same time.

Amil was lost, her mother and Iris were talking above her

head, and that was something she did not like. She looked at her mother. “So Iris has to have surgery?”

Falisa nodded. “Yeah, it’s time for her to get a new look.”

Amil looked at Iris. “A new look wouldn’t hurt.”

# 15

The following day, Aston Oliver landed at Miami International. He was a tall Brazilian in his late forties, physically fit and tanned. His hair was bleach blond and pulled into a neat ponytail that hung just below the nape of his neck. Aston was casually dressed today, and accompanied by a female and male assistant. They were handsomely dressed as well.

The trio grabbed their bags from the baggage claim belt and headed outside into the Florida heat. Aston moved gracefully, his long arms moved in rhythm with his steps. When he got to the curb, his assistants were standing on each side of him. The glare from the sun caught his eyes. He squinted and slipped on an expensive pair of Armani sunglasses.

Just then, a long double stretch limousine pulled up and stopped in front of them, sparkling like a diamond underneath the sun. When the rear window came down, Falisa's face appeared. Her eyes were hidden behind a pair of big black Gucci shades, and she wore a black silk Gucci scarf draped over her head. She held it pinched together underneath her chin.

"Dr. Oliver?" she said politely.

Aston smiled. His teeth were snow white and even. With a slight bow, he answered, “Si, Mrs. Sanchez.”

Falisa smiled back, then her window rolled up and she opened the door from the inside, while the driver went to the rear and loaded their luggage in the trunk. When Aston and his two associates got into the rear of the limousine, Falisa introduced them to Iris.

Aston looked at Iris long and hard, studying the structure of her face. He took his hands and brushed her hair back. He turned her face from one side to the other. He studied the size of her nose, her lips, and even her eyes. Then he took both hands and massaged her cheekbones. Everyone was quiet inside the limousine, and Iris’ heart pumped wildly inside her chest, while the stranger rotated her neck.

The limousine pulled out into traffic, and Aston’s face turned from serious into a smile. He gave Iris an impressed stare, then he looked at Falisa. “Si, Mrs. Sanchez, I owe your husband a hundred favors. This will be some of my best work.”

Falisa smiled at him. “What about her fingerprints?”

Aston grabbed Iris’ hands and looked at them briefly. “No problem,” was all he said.

“A good job, you get a quarter million dollar bonus. An excellent job, you’ll get a half a million dollar bonus,” she said seriously.

“Si, get the half million ready.” He looked Falisa dead in her eyes.

TWO MONTHS HAD PASSED, and Falisa was ready to take her family on a trip. This wasn’t an ordinary trip. Today, Falisa was taking everybody on a trip with the yacht club. Unfortunately, Iris couldn’t join them, but for good reason. Falisa didn’t have her own yacht, but Pepé did, and everything he had was basically hers. When the yacht was set for sail, there were at least ten other yachts sailing out with her. Each owner was a member of the yacht club that Falisa had started.

Today, she just wanted to cruise the ocean with the family. They all sat in an exclusive room that was decorated with fine white marble across the floor, and glass walls that overlooked the ocean. Oversized leather furniture was set up in multiple configurations. Waiters brought them breakfast, which only consisted of fruit platters and freshly squeezed Florida orange juice. Falisa had them to bring out well-done steak strips and toasted bread for the men. She wasn't hungry at all. Something else was on her mind.

She excused herself and took Amil with her. They walked upstairs and outside, to catch the beautiful view of Miami from the large, open decks. They wore matching sundresses and wide straw hats. Amil adored her mother. They stared out into the sparkling blue water in silence, both lost in their own thoughts. Falisa had a lot on her plate, yet she still had more room. The family had to eat, and she would definitely make sure of that. The men that kidnapped her daughter would pay, just as she had made Timbo pay.

She was caught between a rock and a hard place by being married to the man that chopped off her son's leg. She knew Fly didn't like it, but for now, he had to deal with it. She would see to it that they didn't cross paths. At least not yet, anyway.

Amil touched Falisa's hand. "What's the matter?"

"Nothing, baby. For once, everything is fine."

Falisa eased her arm around Amil's neck and then kissed her on the cheek. Falisa took a deep breath, taking in the salty air. Amil did the same.

~

The day had turned to night, and the ocean breeze had turned chilly. Falisa was now in her own private room resting in a hot Jacuzzi on a cordless phone talking to Pepé and massaging her clit underneath the water. She whispered her favorite phrase in his ear. "Si sweet Georgia peach, Pepé."

"Si," he said from the other end. Then there was silence.

Falisa knew he was masturbating, so she just sat back in the water and held the phone pressed against her face and listened to his Spanish whispers and moans. The jets underneath the water massaged her body and helped to ease the tension. She touched her nipples and opened her legs wider.

She whispered again, "Sweet Georgia peach, Pepé."

"Ohh, Falisa," he whispered. "You're the best."

Just on the other side of the door, Amil was eavesdropping on her mother's conversation. She couldn't really hear everything, but she heard enough. She pressed her ear against the door and gave a disappointed look when she couldn't hear more.

Then, without warning, the door came opened and Amil fell to the floor at her mother's feet. Falisa was wrapped in a silk robe decorated with Japanese women holding hand fans. She stared down at Amil for a moment, and then she extended her hand and helped her up.

Falisa closed the door and faced Amil. "Never allow yourself to be labeled as sneaky or nosy. If it is something that you want to know about me, Amil, all you have to do is ask."

Amil stared at her mother. "I just feel that when I'm told the truth, it's still a lie." She walked over toward the dresser and looked at herself in the mirror. Falisa's reflection was behind her. "I just wanna know what happened to my father. That's all I ask."

Falisa knew that she couldn't tell Amil that her father was dead because he'd had her kidnapped, or because he was the reason that her brother had one leg. She couldn't tell her that because of him, she had to turn herself in to be a sex slave. No, she wouldn't dare tell her, because she knew how Amil felt about Timbo.

Falisa walked up to Amil and brushed her hair away from her face. Staring into Timbo's deadly eyes through the mirror, Falisa said in a low whisper. "Your father escaped from the feds and disappeared off the face of the earth. His face is all over America's Most Wanted—"

"I saw it," Amil whispered, then added, "along with Iris. Were they together?"

"Oh no baby, they never met. Timbo is probably on an island somewhere sipping a signature cocktail and laughing at the feds."

Amil smiled, her teeth white and even. "Eating seafood tacos, you know he loved seafood tacos."

Falisa's heart tightened, and it felt as if she'd been punched in the stomach. She hated to lie to her daughter, but at the moment, they were playing the game at an all-time high. Millions of dollars were at stake, as well as a lot of lives. She had two words on her heart for Timbo. *Fuck You!*

# 16

Nearly twenty-four hours had passed, and Falisa's yacht was docked off the coast of Cuba along with twelve other yachts. Falisa mingled with rich white people, and had wine tasting ceremonies. She smoked big Havana cigars with the Cubans, and played golf with an older Asian lady.

While she did all that, Fly, Smurf, Pig Man and Papa Bear were having dinner on another yacht amongst an elite social circle of men in suits and ties. They all sat at a long glossy wood table. Everyone was accepted, regardless of race or religion. All anyone knew was that they were members of the same yacht club. Expensive Cuban cigars were being passed around on silver trays. The best wines and champagnes were poured into long stem glasses.

Tonight's entrees were Sashimi Grade Yellow Fin Tuna, and Captain Cut Rib-eye steaks. A tall model appeared in a long elegant white dress. She was tanned, her lips were painted a bright red, and her eyes were blue. She sat down on the lap of the old looking white man who sat at the head of the long table.

"Everybody, please. Give a round of applause for this lady here. This is the most expensive piece of pussy, I've ever eaten."

Everyone laughed and began to clap. A few whistles came from the table. Fly stood up and clapped louder than the others, until he made eye contact with her. She smiled at him, and then he sat down and paid her no attention. He moved his dreads away from his face and finished dinner.

FALISA HAD INSTRUCTED her crew members to pull out while the rest of the Yachts stayed behind. She checked her watch from the top floor patio. The crisp wind blew through the night. She knew she had to be precise, because Pepé had drummed it in her head. *Timing is everything, baby.* The words were still in her ears.

She at the table with Amil next to her, eating expensive chocolate, and smiling. "Where are we going without Fly and everybody?"

"Just about ten miles out, then we'll turn around and come back." She lifted a half-filled glass of Moet and Chandon and stared hard at her daughter. "What do you want to do after college?"

Amil bit into a piece of chocolate. "I'm not going to college, Mother. Someone has to stay around and look after you, and who is better suited to do it than me? And besides, I'm studying on a college level now."

Falisa sat quietly, taking in every word that her daughter spoke. She sipped from her glass again, and continued to stare at her daughter. They talked back and forth for the next twenty minutes until one of the crew members came and pulled Falisa outside to the rear of the yacht. They were out in the middle of the ocean, and the lights from the yacht illuminated the waters around them.

The captain also came and spoke with Falisa. "The submarine is just below us."

"Send down the fishing nets," was all she said, still holding her glass of champagne.

She followed them outside where two other men were rolling a huge fishing net under the water. Nearly fifty feet underneath them was a five million dollar submarine that Pepé and his brothers owned. They'd sent some men to drop off fifteen hundred kilos of cocaine that was wrapped airtight and waterproof. Two Colombians were under the water when the submarine started spitting out the bricks, three hundred at a time. The Colombians were in scuba diving uniforms and wore night vision goggles. When the first three hundred shot from the tail of the sub, they grabbed the bail by the thick ropes and pulled it up to the fishing nets underneath Falisa's yacht. They loaded the big block into the net, and then they tugged on it.

The crew members pulled up the net by a pulley rotating mechanism. The first bundle weighed over six hundred pounds. When the big square block hit the floor, they all looked at Falisa for further direction.

She sipped from her glass again, and with a quick point of her finger, she said, "It's four more of them down there."

Without a word, they removed the net from the three hundred kilos and tossed it back into the water. By the time they brought up the last three hundred, Falisa was in possession of fifteen hundred bricks of cocaine, and Amil was watching her every move.

When her yacht arrived back at the Cuban docks, Fly, Smurf, Pig Man and Papa Bear were waiting for her. She finally had a chance to relax as they were sailing back to Miami. She asked Fly what city he wanted, and he said Georgia. A city wasn't big enough for him, he needed a state. Pig Man chose Alabama, and Smurf told her he would work the Carolinas,

North and South. Papa Bear was neutral and flexible. Wherever they needed him, he didn't mind.

# 17

A week later, Fly and Smurf were back in Augusta with three hundred keys stashed in the ground on Papa Bear's farm. They rode through the hoods in a rental car, looking for action. They'd kept their ears to the streets to see who was moving the majority of the weight. There were names ringing heavily throughout the CSRA, as it was called. Smurf took down the names and numbers of the few heavyweight brick guys.

At the home of Smurf's mother, Fly waited in the car and talked on his cell phone while looking at himself in the rearview mirror. He looked over the yard and thought back to how all of this had started, the morning Papa Bear and Pig Man pulled up with the three bodies in the trunk of the deuce & a quarter. He even remembered the cereal he was eating from the cup. A female was telling him how much she missed him from the other end, but he wasn't paying that any attention.

"Alright," he said, and hung up the phone.

He looked through the front windshield when he saw Smurf come out the back door. He wore baggy denim jeans, a white T, and all-white Air Force Ones on his feet. Behind his dreads that hung loosely into his face, Fly could see in his eyes that something was wrong. When he jumped into the driver's seat, he took a deep breath and looked at Fly.

"Man, this nigga Six done fucked up." He looked in the rearview mirror and put the shift in reverse, while shaking his head side to side in total disgust.

"What happened?" Fly asked.

Smurf backed out into the street, dug into his front pocket, and removed the folded article from a newspaper. He handed it over to Fly.

He unfolded it and began to read the article.

Anthony Livingston Jr., three months old, died from a broken neck after being severely shaken at his home. His father, Anthony "Six" Livingston, a former basketball all-star for T.W. Josey High School, and the #1 draft pick for the June draft in New York City was charged with murder. Authorities said Mr. Anthony "Six" Livingston Sr. was home alone with the infant, and said he was only trying to stop the baby from crying.

When Fly finished reading the clipping, he looked up at Smurf. "Now I thought I was a stupid ass nigga." He could only shake his head and feel sorry for their old friend. "Who he had a baby by?"

Smurf pulled to a stop sign at Martin Luther King and Tenth avenue. "You remember the lil chick, Jewel, right?"

"Nooo, not the lil cutie?"

They rode in silence for the next twenty minutes, thinking about their old friend's situation. Smurf wouldn't let him down though, that's just the type of dude he was, regardless of the situation.

Smurf would pay for him a lawyer and support the family in way he could. In his heart, he was gonna do what any real friend would do. Over the course of three days, they'd moved seventy bricks between Augusta, Statesboro, Wrens, and Aiken,

South Carolina. He could afford to take care of whatever was necessary.

THE FOLLOWING EVENING, a large U-Haul truck headed down I-20 East, escorted by two rental cars. One of the cars was leading, with the other car in the rear. They moved swiftly through the mild traffic as they exited I-20 onto Turner Hill road. Within minutes, the driver in the first car was punching in his personal security code on the pad in front of a storage company. The automatic chain link fence began to roll back, to allow them entrance. The two cars and the U-Haul eased into the maze of storage bins, bypassing bin after bin.

The first car came to a halt, and Fly stepped out of the passenger side with a key in his hand. He walked up to the bright orange garage type door, unlocked it, and pulled it up. He spun around and waved at the driver of the truck. The driver caught his signal through the rearview mirror and backed up to the front of the bin.

Fly held his hand up and stopped him only four inches away. He went to the truck, grabbed the nylon straps of the steel ramp, and carefully pulled it out until it rested on the concrete. Fly walked up the ramp, unlocked the rear door, and raised it up. The back of the truck was filled with home appliances, mostly refrigerators, washing machines and dryers by Kenmore. When he looked at his watch, it read, 7:43. By 8:28, the rear of the truck was empty and everything had been neatly stacked inside the storage bin.

When they finished, they were back on the move again.

IN ATLANTA, they'd brought five hundred additional kilos of cocaine into the metro area. Later that evening, a candy apple red S-Class Mercedes with chrome rims and Alabama plates pulled into valet parking at the Cheesecake Factory off Peachtree. When the driver's door opened, an older looking man stepped out in slacks, Stacey Adams, and a linen shirt underneath a mid-length mink jacket. Within a few minutes, he was being escorted to a table where Smurf and Pig Man were already waiting. Smurf looked him up and down, just as he was taking a seat. The stranger was in his early fifties and wore his hair cut low, with neatly trimmed facial hair.

Pig Man knew him prior to today, and stuck his hand out. "Hi you doin?"

The older man went by the name Candy Man, and he was known throughout the entire state of Alabama. He shook Pig Man's hand and squeezed it firmly. "I'm A-1 fam'. How 'bout yourself?"

Pig Man nodded. "Everything's everything."

The maître d' came out with a bottle of Cristal on ice and three long stem champagne glasses. The table was set, the bottle was popped, and the maître d' poured the glasses.

"So what's the deal on the white squares, young blood?" Candy Man asked Pig Man.

Pig Man wasn't holding any verbal conversation period, but everything he wanted to say to him, he'd written it down on paper. This was a strategy that Falisa had come up with, in case a conversation was being recorded. He slid the piece of paper to Candy Man.

I got the blocks for twelve grand a piece. If you can produce a million cash, I'll give you one hundred, and an additional one hundred on your face card for an extra one point two million.

When he finished reading, he looked up at Pig Man and then took a few sips from the champagne glass. When he was about to say something, Pig Man hushed him by placing his finger against his lips.

Candy Man gave a confused look. His eyes moved to Fly when he noticed him removing an ink pen from his pocket. He handed it over to him along with a napkin to write on. Pig Man pointed to it, and Candy Man began to write. He bored the tip of the pen against the napkin as if he was trying to dig a hole into it. When he finished, he handed the paper and pen to Pig Man.

We talking big numbers, and I wasn't expecting to be negotiating nothing more than 50 bricks. Not like I don't have the money or nothing like that. Basically, what I'm saying is that my people back home need more insurance. Like family members info, phone numbers and family photos. The school your kids go to.

Pig Man looked up at him. He was impressed by far. He definitely didn't think the Bama boys were on top of it like that. When Pig Man turned the napkin over, he began to write. What he had to say was quick. He slid the paper back to Candy Man.

Even swap ain't no swindle.

Candy Man agreed. They shook hands and ate a nice meal. After a few more drinks, they were in the parking lot. Tomorrow, they will have made a million dollars profit, and would blow it by tomorrow night.

# 18

It actually took them a little over a week to blow the seven figures. They wanted to throw Falisa the biggest party that she would ever see in her lifetime. The Ritz-Carlton-Buckhead was chosen because of its elegance and grand aura. They rented the entire top floor for their immediate friends and family to stay overnight, and ordered the best food and champagne that money could buy.

Their guest list consisted of local rappers like Big Boi from Outkast, players from the Hawks NBA team. Several R&B groups came out along with their managers and security teams. Street millionaires from New York to Texas were there. Amil located everyone through their agents and managers. Running names from the internet was something that she was definitely good at, but when she invited a lady from Paris who had her own exclusive women's clothing line, they were all in shock.

When Fly asked how she got her to come, she simply replied, "Relax and enjoy the party, darling."

Fly thought about that as he looked around the ballroom at over three hundred people who were dressed in everything, including Gucci, Dolce & Gabbana, Versace and Yves Saint

Laurent. Several women were dressed in tailor made women's tuxedos. Anybody that was somebody was there. Fly was in his own lane, dressed in cocaine white leather pants, Louis Vuitton leather loafers and a matching belt, he wore his wife beater tucked in his pants and a soft butter leather jacket with a huge gold plated LV on his back. He moved through the sea of people, shaking hands and mingling here and there.

In the front of the huge room, was something underneath a velvet cover. It stood nearly twelve feet tall. He looked up at it while a guy in a three piece suit asked him, "What's underneath it?"

Fly looked at him, then shook his dreads away from his eyes. Staring at the guy briefly, he said, "Just watch."

A waitress passed by with a tray full of champagne glasses, and he grabbed one before she could stop. She faded away into the crowd, and Fly noticed Smurf heading towards him looking like a million dollars in white on white everything.

He stopped in front of Fly and gave him some dap and a brief hug. "We in the major leagues now," he said.

Fly smiled and nodded his head, then checked his watch. Time was winding down and it was nearing time for Falisa to make her grand entrance. He looked Smurf in the eyes. "I'm going upstairs to check on Amil."

A voice came through the intercom, telling both of them to come to the front entrance of the hotel. Fly looked at Smurf. "She just arrived."

Smurf rubbed his hands together, eagerly anticipating Falisa's arrival. They turned and moved through the crowd until they found the entrance that led to a carpeted hallway, and continued on toward the huge lobby. When they made it to the front of the hotel there were people standing in crowds and casually dressed. Limousines were back to back, music was playing from all directions. Then a long white double stretch Hummer muscled its way toward the entrance. Velvet ropes were set up and hotel security cleared the path where the red carpet was laid.

Fly whispered to Smurf. "Where's the after party?"

"The Platinum House."

The night air was chilly, but boss women and men came out anyway to show homage and respect to somebody that they didn't know from a can of paint. The crowed began to gather, but not coming further than the velvet ropes.

When the Hummer finally stopped, Fly went to the rear door and opened it. When he saw his mother in her all-white gown and heels, he could do nothing but flash a bright smile.

Falisa looked around before stepping down. She saw the paparazzi teams lurking. That satisfied her, because she was the one that called them and paid to have then here. Falisa was indeed in her own lane. The way she thought and did things was totally different from the rest of the world. In her mind, she was equal to the queens from the 1500's and 1600's, but on a modern day scale. She liked mansions in South Beach, a Colombian drug lord husband, and a team of killers who responded to her command only.

When she extended her hand out to Fly, her diamond ring sparkled. He took it and the cameras began to flash as he escorted her down. A guy in the rear of the limousine handed Fly a full length white mink and he draped it over his mother's shoulders.

She faced him with a smile and he gave her a satisfied look. "I had to do something for you," he smiled while holding her hand.

Smurf walked up to her. He loved her like his own mother, and admired her for her strength and loyalty. They hugged briefly and both boys escorted her inside the hotel.

When they made it to the ballroom, she received a standing ovation over the music that bumped through the speakers. There were velvet ropes lined down the middle of the ballroom floor, and they took the carpet up to the front and went straight on the stage. Fly took her mink and Smurf handed her a cordless microphone. They both stepped down and gave her the stage.

Falisa cleared her throat, held her diva stature, and continued to smile. "Good evening kings and queens, dons and divas... and or pawns and bitches. Don't let my words offend any of you, because I'm here to uplift you, whatever your status may be." She paused and stared out into the audience. She now had their undivided attention. They were quiet. "This night is very special to me, because I'm really not supposed to be here. But through the strength of God and myself, Here I am. My words will be short and brief. I am a woman with high standards, and a huge fan of Maya Angelou."

The crowd erupted with whistles and loud applause at the mention of Maya Angelou's name. Falisa smiled and waited for the noise to settle. She walked like a supermodel in her high heels from one end of the stage to the other; she definitely had them.

She placed the microphone up to her mouth, and in a whispered tone, she said, "I don't know if even today, I always like myself. But what I learned to do many years ago, was to forgive myself. It is very important for every human being to forgive him or herself, because if you live, you will make mistakes. It is inevitable. But once you see the mistake, then you forgive yourself and say, 'Well if I'd known better, I'd have done better.' That's all. So you say to people you think you may have injured, 'I'm sorry,' and then you say to yourself, 'I'm sorry.' If we all hold on to the mistake, we can't see our own glory because we have the mistake between our face and the mirror. We can't see what we're capable of being. You can ask forgiveness of others, but in the end, the forgiveness is in one's own self.

"I think that young men and women are so caught up by the way they see themselves. Now mind you, when a large society sees them as unattractive, as threats, as too black or too white or too poor or too fat or too thin or too sexual or too asexual, that's rough. But you can overcome that. The real difficulty is to overcome how you think about yourself. If we don't have that, we never grow, we never learn, and sure as hell we should never teach."

Falisa paused while staring out into the audience. They were captivated. Then she went on, "That one quote alone has made me the queen that I am today. Know yourself, kings and queens. I wanna thank you all for coming out tonight. Now give yourself a round of applause and enjoy yourself."

When she stepped off the stage, the crowd went into an uproar. Women came up and embraced her with warm hugs. Men greeted her with handshakes and lustful looks. Some of them thought they were impressing her with their attire and jewelry, some flashed their veneer white teeth. In exchange, she flashed the same expensive smile.

One lady pulled up in front of Falisa, standing six feet tall in heels and casually dressed. She looked Falisa in her eyes. "If you don't mind me asking, what was your meaning behind the Maya Angelou quote?"

Falisa studied her for a minute, nearly looking into her soul. She gave the stranger a smile, and then she hugged her and whispered in her ear. "Nobody is perfect, baby. The past is the past, and it can't be changed. We all have sinned and done things we're ashamed of. My story and past is unexplainable. Maya's words have pulled me through when I was at my all-time low. Always remember this, you will never know how strong you are if your strength is never challenged." Falisa kissed her cheek.

The lady smiled and continued to stare her in her eyes. "I've never heard nothing like that before," she said.

"It's in you just as well, baby. Fuck what the people say and live your life."

# 19

Fly got the audience's attention and turned everyone toward the huge figure underneath the velvet cover. He grabbed one end and Smurf had the other end. Falisa was standing in front of it as they removed the cover. The huge exclusive ice sculpture was of Falisa sitting on her throne, her hand rested on carved lion heads and her head and eyes were looking straight ahead.

Falisa stared in pure amazement. The ice sculpture of her sitting on a throne was something she hadn't seen before. She covered her mouth with her hands. Fly started to clap and the rest of the crowd followed with loud thunderous applause. All hail the queen.

Bystanders stood next to her and stared at the huge figure. Some looked at her harder to see if it was her face on the ice sculpture. While the party continued, Falisa went upstairs to join Amil in the suite. Inside, Amil was brushing her hair in the mirror while listening to soft classical music that sounded like a live orchestra.

Amil closed the door and faced her mother with a smile,

while continuing to brush her hair. "I'm glad you finally came up, Mother."

Falisa's antennas went up. Her face muscles eased, then she asked, "What's wrong?" she began to move closer toward Amil.

"Did you know that Queen Elizabeth's mother was beheaded when she was three, and King Henry considered his own daughter a bastard?" She sat the brush down and hugged Falisa. "I'm not gonna let anybody hurt you, Mother."

"Well, I'm glad you're gonna protect me, sweetheart." Falisa said as they separated and Amil went to the table and sat down.

She stared at Falisa long and hard. "Queen Elizabeth went to prison also. Her sister was lame for sending her, but when she came home, she became one of the most powerful queens in England. Just like you are today, Mother." She paused and took a deep breath. "So will I be next in line after Fly?"

Amil was smarter than Falisa knew. She'd studied nearly every subject about nation rulers, kings and queens, strategies of war, and Italian mafia lifestyle. She cursed Ivan the Terrible for two weeks straight and she was becoming agitated because Fly hadn't caught up with Hawk yet.

"So, Princess Amil," Falisa said and began taking off her shoes. One at a time she handed them to Amil. "Try them on."

Amil took the expensive white heels and carefully placed them on her feet. Then she stood up, now standing four inches taller. Amil stared at her.

"Now let me see you walk in them."

"Where, just around the room?" Amil asked confused.

Falisa nodded.

Amil tried walking in the uncomfortable heels, her left foot turned to the side a little. She looked back at her mother. "They feel funny."

"I know, just keep walking."

"Where?"

"In my shoes."

"I'm in your shoes, Mother. Do I walk in circles?"

"If you're in my shoes, you should know that I don't walk in circles."

Amil was on the other side of the room trying to strike a pose in the heels. "I don't get it."

"How do you not get it? And you're asking for a queen position?"

Amil sat down next to her.

"No, get up. You'll walk all night in those shoes until you know where you wanna go."

Amil almost given her that stare, but she caught herself and flashed a smile instead. She stood up and walked around the hotel room in silence. She thought long and hard as she moved. Nearly fifteen minutes passed, and Amil was still walking in silence. Falisa didn't know how mad she was, and she definitely didn't show it on her face. Another fifteen minutes passed and Amil stopped and looked at her. "This is ridiculous Mother, and these shoes are really starting to get uncomfortable."

"Take them off."

Amil sat down and removed the high heels from her feet.

"Now put them back on." Falisa's voice was calm and polite.

Again, Amil looked at her mother. She held her tongue and put the shoes back on. She stood up and Falisa told her to walk. As she began moving around the room again, Falisa spoke. "Life won't give you a break, baby. And walking in my shoes could definitely be uncomfortable." Falisa paused. "You get where I'm coming from?"

"Not really," Amil said. She paused and put her hands on her hips.

Falisa beckoned Amil with her finger, telling her to come and sit next to her. Amil sat down, and Falisa put her arm around her neck. "It's two sides to every coin, baby. And that statement goes for people also. Let me tell you the other side, okay? And what I mean by walking in my shoes."

Amil definitely wanted to hear this. She sat back and crossed her legs, ears tuned in. This is what she had been waiting for.

# 20

The day Dr. Aston Oliver changed Iris' face and removed her fingerprints, it changed her life. After two months of healing, she and Falisa had devised a plan. First off, they came up with an alias for Iris, and another one for back-up. They created a third one for full coverage insurance, as a last resort.

This morning, she went by the name Olivia Gardner. She was forty years old, and a graduate of UCLA. She had all the official paperwork to show her achievements and credentials, and a background saying her mother and father owned oil tanks and wells in Nottingham, Pennsylvania. She knew the average Joe in the streets couldn't talk the 'Drilling for Oil' language. That was another league. Maybe recording studios, restaurants, clubs, or detail shops, but not oil. So today, Olivia Gardner was a sophisticated black woman, the daughter of a millionaire family and an attorney herself.

She had her own one bedroom apartment in a high-rise building in downtown Manhattan. Iris' body was still petite, and her dark skin was smooth. Her lips were much fuller, her nose was altered a little, and the bone structure of her jaw and chin had been changed. She wore honey colored contact lenses, that couldn't be removed unless Dr. Oliver did it himself. Iris wore her new hair implant like it was hers.

Casually dressed in a two-piece pants suit and expensive clear lens glasses, Iris stood at the mini wet bar and poured herself a drink. She looked at herself in the wall mirror and smiled. Her new set of teeth were veneers and very impressive looking. She loved the new look, and she knew her new date would like her.

After she sipped from her glass, she turned around to the huge living room where white leather furniture, white elephant tusk and white marble floor filled her eyesight. A man sat on the sofa twirling a cigar in his mouth, while looking over an income statement from her family business.

Iris walked over to him, her heels click clacking against the marble. The guy had a bottle of champagne on the table in front of him. He turned up the bottle with his dysfunctional hand. Iris sat next to him and kissed his cheek.

"So what do you think?" she asked him.

He turned toward her. "So all you need is someone to run the club here in New York?"

"You keep saying club. It's not a club. Use the word social setting or something. More casual, you know. Polo Country Club in New York, black owned." She touched his chest with a long manicured nail. "And you're gonna be that manager."

"I'm with that, Olivia. I've been looking for something legit to get into anyway. So how do we get started?"

"We'll fly down to Georgia, no further than Atlanta. I'll let you meet my parents—"

"I really don't do the Georgia scene at all, ma," he cut her off.

Olivia looked at him, confused. She sipped from her glass. "You'll only be in Atlanta for one day. I hate going down there also, especially after the Olympics last year." She turned his face toward hers and their eyes met. "One day, and we're back."

He agreed, simply nodding his head. Then he asked. "How are we flying, Delta?"

He turned up the champagne, brought it down, and Olivia took it from him. She turned it up and took a swallow. "Mother will send her jet, I'm sure." She leaned in and kissed his cheek. "Stop being camera shy."

FALISA HAD SENT the jet to New York to pick up Olivia and her new business partner. They were now landing at Daniel Fields airport in Augusta. He looked out the window as the private jet's wheels screeched against the asphalt. "This don't look like Atlanta," he said, then turned his head toward Olivia and waited for her to respond.

"My uncle owns this airstrip. Our drive will be short." She flashed him a confident smile and dropped her eyes down to her Cartier wristwatch. "What do you want for lunch?"

"Lobster and Fettuccini, red wine, and a Cuban cigar," His eyes squinted as if he wanted to say something else. *Fuck it, why not?* He thought. "And a rich bitch to top me off for dessert." He grabbed his wood through his jeans, giving Iris an easy line to read between to understand that he wanted some head after lunch.

With her confident and impressive smile, she whispered. "I'm sure I can arrange that."

Iris removed her seatbelt and stood up. She picked up a small leather Gucci bag. When she eased her hand inside, she grabbed a high voltage taser gun. Casually, she pulled her hand from the bag and aimed the taser at him. Strings of needlepoint wire shot from her hand and hit him in his chest. He jumped instantly at the shocking, horrible pain that raced through his body. He yelled out as he tried to fight it, then his body suddenly went limp.

She removed the needle wire from his tee shirt. Papa Bear came into the cabin dressed in his usual working gear; a Dickie overall suit and gloves. He removed the seatbelt from Ox, picked him up, and slung him over his shoulder. When they exited the plane, they stuffed Ox in the rear of a blue service van with a bogus Carpet Cleaner logo painted on the side. Papa Bear bound his ankles with a plastic tie, and another one around his wrist. He checked his hand where his fingers were missing. Then he checked his pulse; he was still alive.

Papa Bear got behind the wheel and Olivia took the passenger side. When they left the airport, they headed to the farm in Harlem, Georgia. When they arrived, they removed Ox from the van and brought him inside the house through the back door. Papa Bear dropped him on the floor, and he sat there with his hands and ankles bound together.

Still a little dazed, he looked around the strange place. Nothing looked familiar to him. He looked up, the ceilings were low and there wasn't any furniture. The floor was made of concrete, and the ceilings were wood. The walls looked to be carefully constructed. Ox took a deep breath and began trying to free his hands from the plastic ties.

Just then, the door opened and Papa Bear entered with a pair of stainless steel shackles in his hand. "Sit tight, warrior." Papa Bear said in a calm voice. He clamped the shackles around his ankles and squeezed them on tight, to the point where if he so much as moved an inch, they would cut into his skin.

Ox squinted, but he didn't respond to the pain. When Papa Bear removed a pair of steel handcuffs from his pocket, Ox held out his bound arms toward him. Papa Bear clamped them on his wrist and looked Ox dead in the eyes. He stood up and slowly began to walk around him, circling the room in total silence.

"Why aren't you wearing your glasses? You've switched to contact lenses since the last time I seen you."

Ox remained silent, his eyes down and now staring at the floor. He could only see Papa Bear's boots as they passed him.

"Over four years, I've studied the tape, the structure of your face behind the ski mask you wore. The small twitch in your left eye, the description we got from the messenger you sent." Papa Bear went silent again, he continued to orbit around him, calmly and slowly, waiting for him to raise his head.

He saw Ox take a deep breath, and then he looked up at Papa Bear with a smile.

# 21

In the next room, Iris was on the phone with Falisa. There was a bright smile across her face as she listened to her on the other end. "Oh, he's definitely intelligent, very good with words." She crossed her legs and waited for Falisa to respond.

"Maybe we can get a seven figure ticket for him. I'm sure he has to be worth something," Falisa said from the other end. She paused, then added, "I mean seriously, for some reason, niggas from New York tend to be so damn stubborn."

"And that I do know, trust me. This dude is a piece of work." Iris said. She took a deep breath. "Let me get back to work, then."

"Okay. I guess you know Fly and Smurf are on the way."

Iris smiled. "I'm sure they are."

"Be safe, love."

"You too." Iris hung up the phone and walked toward the room where Papa Bear and Ox were.

~

INSIDE A WELL-DESIGNED recording studio in lower Manhattan, Hawk sat comfortably in his high backed leather swivel chair. He sipped Courvoisier from a glass and twisted the ashes from a blunt into an ashtray. The studio was furnished tastefully with a leather circular sofa, thick carpet, cherry oak and several paintings and photos of his late idol, Jean-Michel Basquiat, the American artist from Brooklyn that started his career with graffiti.

He listened to a slow instrumental beat through a pair of earphones as he looked at a new female artist through a glass recording booth. She had no musical talent whatsoever, but she had the prettiest face and nicely shaped body. He shook his head, trying to conceal his frustration. He stood from his chair and tapped the glass of the recording booth. The girl turned and faced him. Looking into his eyes, she noticed the frustration. She politely brushed her hair away from her eyes with her hand, then she smiled.

"C'mere." he said and motioned his hand.

Her smile slightly faded. She stepped out of the booth and walked up to him. "Listen," he said calmly. "You're in a recording studio, not the Grand Canyon. You do not have to scream into the microphone. You only do that shit when you start the second verse."

She was small with almond shaped eyes, and was dressed in a Michael Jordan jersey and a pair of small shorts.

She looked Hawk in his eyes. "I'm tired, Papi." she whispered softly.

"So, I'm not supposed to be tired?" he shouted, then added in a lower tone. "Listen, Star. Let's get this out the way." He turned and looked at his sound engineer across the room. "Son, let her know how she's gonna look front row at the BET Award."

The guy behind the sound board said, "Word. Pretty face, phat ass, you'll get an award."

She smiled shyly, turned around and headed back into the studio. The door closed, and Hawk got his blunt from the ashtray and sipped his drink. When he finally placed his earphones on his head, his cell phone vibrated in his front pocket. He pressed his lips together to suppress his anger, and then retrieved his phone from his front pocket. According to his Rolex, it was a little past two a.m. He stared at the screen. The incoming number was private.

Although he didn't know who was calling him, he finally pressed the send button and answered. "What's good?"

"Peace!"

"Peace!" Hawk replied back. He sipped his drink and focused his eyes on the girl in the recording booth.

"Hawk, what up, son? This Ox."

Hawk turned his attention back to the phone conversation. "Hi you, Ox? Damn it's been a minute."

"We got a situation, son."

"I'm listening."

"Niggas got me in Georgia, yo."

Hawk gave Ox his undivided attention now. He drained his glass of Courvoisier and quickly sat it down. "What are you doing down there, son?"

"Listen God," Ox said in a low, deep tone, "the situation with your people down here a few years ago. They're responsible for Cory and his mother, and they have me here for a ransom."

Hawk's eyes went back to the girl in the booth. He envisioned her naked, the smell of her peppermint laced breath, and her tiny nipples. "Word," he said, rubbing his hand over his face. He took a deep breath, then asked, "What's the ransom fee?" He was hoping they didn't demand anything over a million dollars. *Okay, two million, and that's the max.* He thought.

"They want your life, God." Ox said. "No funds on this

round. But yo, this is the deal. They're not gonna play fair son. I'm here now. Take care of my sons and my queen."

"Are you serious, God?" Hawk asked. Then he stood up with a frown. "Let 'em know I got two million available to be transferred to where ever, son."

There was a short silence, then Ox responded. "On my word just...."

The line disconnected.

Hawk looked at his phone and thought about his comrade's situation long and hard. He knew they would kill him if they caught him. However, Hawk wasn't a pushover, and he was treacherous just like his father. He would retaliate in due time, and he would go hard. When he looked toward the booth again, his vision was blurred. He picked up the phone and made a call to some certified henchmen in Brooklyn. He told them what the problem was, and hung up. He then called some more people to pick up Ox's family. He would have them moved out to the Hamptons where he lived quietly and peacefully.

Timbo flashed before his eyes. His words from years ago rang in his ears. *Never under estimate Georgia. It's some thoroughbred niggas down here.*

# 22

When Smurf pulled out of the Formula 1 parking lot in his new glossy black Lamborghini, the engine was screaming in one gear and roaring like a monster in another. He fish tailed out into Piedmont, and behind him, Fly had the tires screeching against the asphalt in an all-white Lamborghini. He almost sideswiped an older lady's Volvo. He straightened up his wheel and followed behind Smurf.

Through the city of Atlanta, they rode and turned heads. On their way toward the West End, Smurf was on his cell phone talking to January as she guided him toward the AV center. When they arrived, the area and scene was crawling with young beautiful college females and a few guys. The females swarmed around both of the Lamborghinis, trying to see inside.

When Smurf opened his driver side door, it rose up like a butterfly wing. The engine was still running when he stepped out. He was dressed in Louis Vuitton boat shoes, jeans and a brown leather Polo jacket.

He noticed January coming through the crowd. Her hair

was pulled into a tight ponytail. She was dressed in a mid-length burgundy jacket, jeans, and leather boots that matched her jacket. When she got a full and close look at Smurf, her face broke out into an overwhelming smile. She embraced him and kissed him as if he'd just returned back from the Dessert Storm war.

"Where in the hell have you been?" she screamed, her arms closing tighter around him.

It's a long story," he whispered in her ear as he held onto her.

Then the driver side door of the Lamborghini that Fly was in rose. When he stepped out, January didn't recognize him at first because of the dreads and his height. Then she covered her mouth with both hands to keep her screams under control. "Oh... My... God... Fly?" she said. "Is that you?"

"Damn right! Who else it's gonna be?" He walked up to January and gave her a hug, then out the corner of his eye, he noticed a tall yellow female with long hair walking past him. "How you been?" he asked January.

"I'm fine." she shot back.

"I'ma catch up in a minute." he told her and Smurf, then he went and caught up with the tall yellow female. She was walking like a model, and Fly was caught up in her shapely body and pretty face. "Excuse Me." he said.

She stopped and turned around. Her eyes had Fly captivated. He walked up to her and extended his hand. She shook it. Then he asked, "You got a minute?"

She flashed a smile, her eyes cut to the Lam and back to him. "Yes." She responded, but that was a understatement. She walked up closer, inches away from his face. "You must be a rapper."

"Yeah, now get in." he told her.

Fly released her hand and went to the driver side where the door was still up. She moved around to the passenger side. Fly opened her door from the inside. It rose skyward and that amazed her. When she got inside, the first thing she did was allow her fingers to trace over the leather interior of the Lamborghini, carefully clawing her manicured nails along the edges of the dashboard.

She looked at Fly. “Is this your car?”

“Yes, it is. But don’t call it a car, please.”

She stared hard at him. “Well, what should I call it?” Her voice was soft and proper, with a northern accent.

“Lesbian. She loves women, and she got your panties wet.”

Fly had her so confused with what he’d just said, she didn’t know how to respond. All she could say was, “Excuse me?”

“Just a joke, beautiful. They call me Fly. And you?”

“Zoë.” she said, and then smiled again.

Fly nodded as if he was impressed. “You in school out here?”

“Of course. I’m at Spelman.”

SMURF GRABBED January by her hand and held it. He pulled her and they began to walk in silence for a moment. On the edge of the grass of the Robert W. Woodruff library, they stopped. “So what’s up with your home girls Jewel and Angel?” Smurf asked her.

“A long story, I guess.” She seemed down when she spoke. Her eyes cut down to the ground. Smurf stopped and faced her. He recognized from her tone of voice that something was on her mind. “Something you wanna talk about?” he asked her.

“Yeah, but not out here.”

“Where you stayin’ at?”

“I’m on Clark campus. We definitely can’t go there.”

“Come with me, let’s go eat and talk.”

She agreed and Smurf escorted her to the passenger side of

his Lamborghini. He walked toward Fly and leaned down. "We going to eat."

Fly nodded. "I'm following you, brah." he said, then looked over at Zoë. "Can I take you out to eat?"

"You can take me where ever you want to." she said with a smile.

WITH TRAFFIC, it took them nearly an hour to get to the Cheesecake Factory across town. They were becoming regulars at this restaurant. They loved the scene, the atmosphere, and the food. As they entered the parking lot, heads turned and people pointed at them as if they were from outer space. One valet went to Smurf's Lam first because he was in front. Another one walked up to Fly and leaned down at his window. "Good afternoon, sir."

Moments later, Smurf and January were walking inside the restaurant, and Fly and Zoë were walking in behind them. During their ride, Zoë had told Fly that she was originally from Missouri and her father was in the military in Columbus, Georgia. They sent her to Spelman to finish her education. She also told him that she has a friend back in Milwaukee, but they only talked on the phone once a week and nothing more. Fly listened at her closely, but he really wasn't interested in her past. Only the future, only her pretty face and phat ass is what he was focused on.

Inside, Smurf and January got their own table, and so did Fly and Zoë. Smurf picked a cozy table in the corner underneath a dim light. January was seated across from him, still looking intelligent and innocent as she did four years ago. Smurf had a soft spot for her for some reason. His hands grabbed hers and he looked her directly in her eyes.

“First question, are you in a relationship with anybody?” he asked her.

“No, your mother told me you was locked up in Florida back in ninety-three.” She paused, then smiled shyly. “So I kind of waited.” She held on to his hands and they stared into each other’s eyes for a moment, realizing how much they missed each other.

A waiter approached, Smurf looked up at him for a brief second. “Jamaican Black Pepper Shrimp.” he told him. Then he looked at January. “What you eating?”

She shrugged lightly, her eyes still fixed on his. Then she looked up at the waiter. “Same thing he ordered.”

“It’s real spicy, now,” Smurf warned her.

She smiled at Smurf and leaned in toward him. “Can I kiss you?” she asked in a soft tone voice.

Smurf leaned in close to her. The smell of cinnamon was on her breath. He allowed his lips to touch hers, then January closed her eyes and her tongue found his. Smurf sucked on her bottom lip, she sucked his top lip hungrily and seductively. Smurf laughed and pulled away from her. She opened her eyes and they had turned moist.

Her face saddened as her final question rolled from her tongue. “Are we gonna be together?”

Smurf’s eyebrows bunched together and he drew his head back slightly and gave her a look as if he couldn’t believe she asked that question. Then he said, “Baby, we together like Ashford and Simpson.”

Her face turned into a smile. “Solid as a rock.”

Smurf leaned in and kissed her a second time, with more passion and finesse.

~

FLY STARED at the menu for a brief moment, then he cut his eyes up at Zoë. "You hungry?" he asked her.

"Yes." She shot back. "I'll have the Herb Crusted Filet of Salmon." Zoë told the waiter.

Fly looked at the menu. "Same thing, hold the asparagus."

"Drinks?" The waiter asked.

"Water for me," Zoë said. "And can we get a bowl of fresh strawberries and whipped cream while we wait?"

"Of course, ma'am." He looked at Fly. "What would you like to drink, sir?"

"Water also."

When he wrote everything down and walked away, Zoë looked square into Fly's eyes. "So, who do you rap for?"

Fly laughed half-heartedly. "Only thing I wrap is rubber bands around money, baby." That was the only way he could describe it.

She smiled and flashed a pretty row of white teeth. *Magazine material for sure.* Fly thought. Then his phone rang.

# 23

Fly pulled his phone from his pocket. "Hello," he answered.

Zoë blew him a playful kiss, and he smiled. When he heard Pig Man's voice on the other end, his smile faded.

"Where you at nigga?"

"Cheesecake Factory."

"Good, I thought you was in some pussy."

Fly smiled at Pig Mans statement and at Zoë the same time. "If I was, I wouldn't have answered the phone."

"When young nigga's nuts get hot, they tend to lose all focus. You talkin' all slick and shit. You must be in the presence of a woman?"

"Man, I'm tryna enjoy myself. What's up?"

"I got a problem, and I need to see you and Smurf like A.S.A.P. But go ahead and eat first, and enjoy yourselves. Ya'll come my way soon as, though."

Fly was still smiling, but on the inside he heard distress in Pig Man's voice. He pressed the end button on his phone, and then he stared at the beautiful piece of work that sat before him. "So, your mom and dad are in Columbus, Georgia?"

Zoë looked at Fly and chirped. "Yes, Fort Benning, but I'd rather talk about you. Where you from?"

"Augusta."

"That's not far from here. Isn't that where James Brown is from?"

Fly laughed. "Yeah."

"What? Why you laughed?" she asked, then reached across the table and rubbed his hand.

"Just trippin', cause when everybody hear Augusta, they automatically think about James Brown."

When their food came, Fly and Zoë talked for nearly another hour and Smurf and January caught up on old times also. He'd finally gotten the story on everyone from her. When Fly got up and walked over to Smurf's table, he whispered in his ear. "We gotta go see Pig Man, I believe he got a situation."

January looked up at him. "Fly, don't think you've grown up and done got too big. I'm still the big sister."

Fly walked around the table to where she was at and gave her another hug. "I'm just handling some business, nothing personal."

She smiled and playfully touched the edge of his dreads. "I love both of your new looks."

"Fly." Smurf said as he stood up next to him. He politely pulled him away from the table out of earshot. "What's up, brah?"

"Pig Man just called me like he had a situation, but he told me to go ahead and eat and stuff. We probably need to make a quick stop over there."

Smurf thought briefly, then he pulled out his own cell phone and punched in Pig Man's number. Pig Man answered on the third ring. "Hello."

"What's good, brah?" Smurf asked.

"Man, listen," Pig Man said, then went on. "Ya'll come see me A.S.A.P." He hung up the phone.

Smurf looked at Fly and nodded his head. "Let's go out here and see what's up with brah."

~

By the time they arrived at Pig Man's stash house, the sky had turned dark gray and thunder was clapping fiercely through the night. Smurf parked his Lamborghini in the first garage and Fly occupied the next garage. The four of them got out inside the damp garage. They took the rear door where Pig Man waited for them with an automatic handgun with an extended clip.

"I didn't know ya'll was bringing company." Pig Man said and allowed the four of them to come inside.

Pig Man closed the door and locked it. He knew January from back when Smurf was younger. Then he looked at Zoë as if he'd seen her somewhere before, but he brushed it off. January and Zoë found a seat in the living room while Pig Man escorted Smurf and Fly to the master bedroom and locked the door.

He turned and faced them. "Rule one, never bring an outsider to our stash house." His eyes went to Fly. "Where you know her from?" He still held the automatic firmly in his hand.

"I just met her. She go to Spelman." Fly said, and then he walked over to the bed and sat down.

He took his pants off and frowned. There was a sharp pain in his leg from the prosthesis. He unstrapped it and rubbed his nub while looking at Pig Man. Pig Man hated when Fly revealed his leg. He couldn't stand to see him in that situation. Pig Man turned and went toward the window. It was pouring rain outside.

He faced Smurf and Fly. "I spoke with Falisa earlier, she informed me that my name came up in a federal indictment," he said, and went underneath the bed and pulled out two large canvas duffle bags with large bills equaling to $2.5 million dollars. One at a time, he lifted the bags on top of the bed. Then he pulled out a mini-electric money counting machine.

"This ain't another one of your jokes is it?" Fly asked.

Pig Man walked toward the dresser, sat his gun down, and picked up a cigarette and a lighter. He began to talk while lighting up the Newport. "Two things I don't play about, one is the police. Two is the police tryin' to apprehend me."

Smurf only nodded his head, then he shrugged. "So where you going?"

"Don't know yet. Falisa got it set up for me, though. She won't even tell me where I'm going."

Fly began strapping his prosthetic back on. Smurf faced him. "How yo' leg feeling?" he asked him.

Fly cringed a little. "Sharp pains. Just came out of nowhere."

"You need to relax for a couple of days or somethin'." Smurf told him.

Pig Man stood up, cigarette smoke curled around his lips. "Take a break lil brah. Take that lil pretty bitch you got to Miami and rest or somethin'."

"She in school at Spelman."

"Go get a suite at the Ritz or somethin'. You need a break." He placed a hand on his shoulder, then he produced a piece of paper with a name and address on it. "Call this number, good dude. Just let him know we on the same team. He knows every street and alley through the whole city of Atlanta."

"So what about this house?" Smurf asked.

"Tonight is my last night here. Whatever yawl wanna do. Jus' don't have no money, no drugs, and no guns up in here and everything should be official."

"When you leaving?" Fly asked, looking up at Pig Man from the bed.

"Now. I jus' had to make sho' yawl got that money and that info. Hopefully, it will be no longer than a year."

Pig Man walked up to Smurf and hugged him. "Be careful, take care of your lil brother," he whispered in his ear.

Fly stood up. He quickly put his pants back on and he and Pig Man embraced. "Yawl niggas gotta stay focused out here."

"We got this end," Fly told him. "You just make sho' you handle your end."

After Pig Man left, Smurf loaded the money up in his Lamborghini and left with January. Fly brought Zoë into the bedroom and they lay down on the bed and talked for the rest of the night. When he told her about his leg, she felt uncomfortable, but she didn't have a problem with it.

"So does it hurt now?" she asked him while they were snuggled up against each other.

"Yeah, a lil bit."

Zoë began to massage his leg for him while lying in the king sized bed. Then she undressed him until he was completely naked. She slowly removed her clothes. Fly stared at her beautiful red nipples. She wore a gold piercing in her navel and had four cat paws tatted on her thigh. Her naked body smelled of Jasmine, which seeped into his nostrils, Fly grabbed the back of her arm and carefully pulled her to him until her firm breasts were pressed against his chest. Their eyes, nose and mouth were no further than an inch apart.

"Zoë." he whispered.

"Yes?" she responded, then she sucked his bottom lip in a slow-slurping movement.

"That's a fly name."

"Meaning it's catchy or do I belong to you?" she smiled, then brushed her nose against his neck and began to grind on his penis, moving her body in a waving motion.

Fly reached and slid her black satin panties to the side and eased his hard penis through the opening of her vagina lips with the other hand. Zoë was leaking between her legs, wet like a water fountain. When she could no longer take the teasing, she grabbed him and forced him inside of her. Fly felt her tight vagina wrap around his penis.

"Good pussy, Zoë." Fly said, looking up at her as she moved.

She was on top of him now, her hands pressing against his chest. She moved slowly, working her vagina muscles. "Is it good? Or are you trying to make me feel good about myself?" she nibbled at his earlobe.

For the next two hours, they had nonstop sex until they laid in each other arms, exhausted. She looked at Fly and whispered, "If your leg is still hurting, I know somebody that sells real good pain pills called Oxycontin."

"Call them. I'll try anything right about now."

# 24

Three days later, Falisa was in Miami at her mansion, swimming laps with Amil in the Olympic swimming pool. They wore twin Burberry bathing suits. Falisa came from underneath the water, holding on to the side of the pool. She wiped the water from her eyes and looked up at Iris relaxing in the poolside recliner chair, sipping on a margarita from a straw and watching them from behind a pair of dark Chanel shades.

"The water is nice, Iris." Falisa said, and pulled herself out of the water.

Iris handed her a thick towel and Falisa wiped her face and took the recliner next to Iris. She placed a pair of matching shades on her eyes from the small table that separated them. She took the margarita from the table, sipped it, and laid back. Without looking toward Iris, she said to her, "Life couldn't be better, baby."

They both watched Amil climb the ladder out of the pool and up to the diving board. She turned around backwards at the edge of it.

"I definitely agree. It's truly a blessing to be here, Falisa."

Amil raised her arms above her head, her body gently curved and tight. "Are y'all paying attention?" Amil asked.

"Cameras rolling baby," Falisa said. She then sat her drink down.

Amil bounced two times and flipped from the diving board, tucked her body into a ball and then quickly opened up, stretched out, and dived perfectly into the water.

Falisa began clapping for her daughter. Iris sat her drink down and joined in with Falisa. They clapped until Amil pulled herself out of the pool. Falisa threw her a towel and she quickly dried her face and wrapped up her head.

"I'm going inside," she said and continued towards the patio doors, leaving Iris and Falisa to themselves.

When Amil got inside and went into her bedroom, she made sure her room door was locked. She walked to her dresser and wall mirror, and paused while removing the towel from her head. She carefully studied her reflection. Amil had it all, the looks, the body, and the brains; however, there were a few screws missing. She wanted to take after Falisa so badly, that she was to the point where she needed to hear every conversation that her mother had with anyone.

A couple of weeks ago, Amil had located a local spy-surveillance shop in Miami that sold illegal listening devices and hidden cameras and wiretaps. She asked the people enough questions to put everything together. She used her mother's credit cards to make the purchase. Last week, while Falisa was in Georgia, Amil called them in to set up the surveillance equipment and made her private bedroom the headquarters. There were over four cameras spread throughout the mansion, and Falisa or anybody else wouldn't detect them because they were phony Hi Res Carbon Monoxide alarms.

The toy that she special ordered for herself was called the Orbitor Electronic listening device. She walked into her closet and removed the gadget from a Nine West shoebox .She placed the cushioned earphones on her head and flipped the "ON" switch on the handheld device. Amil opened her window just enough to aim the device downstairs toward Falisa and Iris. She quickly began listening in on their conversation.

IRIS: I wonder how long Fly is planning to let Ox stay alive.

Amil eyebrows bunched together. She definitely wasn't expecting to hear that, and she instantly turned angry. She tuned in and aimed the microphone directly at her mother.

FALISA: I'm not sure, but I am going to trust his judgment on this. It has to be something that he has that can benefit us. Other than that, he is wasting air here on earth. I mean, some niggas really aren't worthy of living, Iris.

IRIS: Well, the best part is that we can kill him anytime we want to.

FALISA: We'll hold him until further notice. He's a loyal son of a bitch, though.

Amil stood in the window overlooking the poolside where her mother and Iris sipped their margaritas in silence. She never removed the headphones from her ears.

IRIS: Conversation is money, time is money. But when it's your life, money is not an option.

Amil wrote that down on a piece of paper. She removed her headphones and placed her listening device back into the shoebox, and with sadness written all over her face, she walked into the bathroom.

Downstairs, Falisa was coming through the kitchen when the house phone rang. She answered the cordless phone from off the marble countertop. "Hello."

"Si, my beautiful wife," Pepé said from the other end.

Falisa smiled and positioned the phone between her neck and shoulder. "Hi Pepé." She chirped his name happily while removing a Tupperware bowl of fruit.

"I'm coming to see you this weekend."

"Wonderful, I'll make arrangements." she said, and walked

to the island countertop and sat the bowl down. "Anything special?"

"Si, Polo Club arrangements."

Falisa smiled. She knew how much Pepé loved to watch a good polo game, smoke cigars, and sip hard liquor on the rocks. Falisa removed the top from the bowl of fruit and casually nibbled on the small tip of a strawberry.

"Anything else, sweetheart?"

"Si, sweet Georgia peach," he said.

Her smile got wider and brighter. "I'll send the Lear for you."

"No... No worry, beautiful. That's yours. I just bought a new one. I'll fly in alone this weekend."

"Will you bring me a gift? Something exclusive for my daughter?"

"I will, see you this weekend." He hung up.

Falisa hung up also, then Iris appeared in the kitchen wrapped in a terry cloth robe with her hair wrapped in a towel.

She stopped in front of Falisa. "I think I'm ready to take your advice."

Falisa gave her a bewildered look, causing her eyebrows to raise in question. "What's that?" she asked.

"I wanna get my breasts done." Iris said.

"What about your ass?" Falisa said. "You definitely need that done also. There's nothing back there, Iris," she said with laughter in her voice.

"Well, I think I'm ready for both of them."

When Falisa finished the half-eaten strawberry, Amil appeared at the doorway, still dressed in her swimsuit and with a towel wrapped around her head.

"I'm glad I got both of you together," Amil said.

Iris and Falisa both turned toward Amil. Then on impulse, Amil snatched the towel from her head and revealed her bald head to them. She'd shaved her head clean except for a few patches of hair.

Falisa frowned and spit the strawberry from her mouth.

"Amil, what the fuck have you done?" Falisa shouted angrily.

Amil stood there with the stupidest looking grin across her face. Then she whispered, "My friend told me to do it."

## 25

At 9:00 the next morning, Falisa arrived at a private doctor's office in downtown Miami, pulling Amil by her hand as if she was a five-year-old little girl. Iris was their escort. When they got inside, the doctor was already waiting for them in a colorful, plush waiting room. He stood when they entered. He appeared to be an intelligent psychiatrist, dressed in gray slacks and a soft gray dress shirt. He flashed a handsome smile and greeted them.

"Good morning," he said and extended his hand. "As you know, I'm Dr. Hollands."

Falisa shook his hand, she didn't smile one bit.

"Hello Dr. Hollands. I'm Mrs. Walker. This is my daughter, Amil."

"Nice to meet you," he said to Falisa and then looked at Amil and extended his hand out to her. Amil shook his hand. Dr. Hollands stared briefly into her eyes and noticed the Louis Vuitton scarf wrapped around her head.

"Good morning, Dr. Hollands." Amil chirped happily. "I'm Amil, the one that's supposed to be crazy, but I'm really not."

Dr. Hollands continued to hold her hand. He looked at Falisa. "I can take her now."

Falisa nodded in agreement. "I'll wait for her in the lobby." She sat down and crossed her legs.

Iris found a seat across from her and grabbed a magazine from the table. She crossed her legs as well and began flipping through a few pages. She was concerned for Amil because she'd been through this before with her, when she was thirteen and while they were living on Papa Bear's farm. Iris had gone into Amil's room, and discovered that she had ripped the heads from all her baby dolls and teddy bears. This was something a little more complex, though.

Falisa spoke and broke her concentration. "I see you're thinking very hard. What's on your mind?"

Iris looked up from the magazine she wasn't paying any attention to. Her eyes met Falisa's eyes, then she slowly shook her head from side to side.

"Amil is such a sweetheart," she said, "and to see her go into her twilight zone don't sit well with me."

"Well, it's not like we're not taking all the right steps. I mean, we were just swimming and relaxing. Then all of a sudden she comes out of nowhere with this... This shaved head bullshit." Falisa was getting angrier by the second, just thinking about how Amil had cut every inch of hair off her head. The thought disgusted her. She took a deep breath. Her eyes were fire red. She took another deep breath, anxiously calming herself down.

"It'll pass over, Falisa," Iris simply said. "But she's also getting older."

There was a long pause. "And that means she'll only get worse." Falisa murmured.

Iris finally closed the magazine and sat it on the table. "We got to mold her, Falisa. She has to be prepared for the world."

Inside Dr. Hollands' office, Amil was laid back across an

expensive leather couch staring at the ceiling. Dr. Hollands was sitting in a chair next to her with a small notepad and an ink pen. "Amil, are you comfortable around your family?" he asked her.

"Am I supposed to be honest when I answer you?"

"I hope you would be honest."

Amil felt the surge of an adrenaline rush run through her veins. "I love my family, Doc." she said, while staring toward the ceiling. "But I have a different outlook on things. It's like, I'm looking at the world through a rearview mirror."

Dr. Hollands wrote that down on his notepad. He was paying close attention to everything she said. He smiled and looked up at her again. "A rearview mirror? I'm assuming you mean that you're always looking behind you. More like paranoia?" he said to her.

Amil took a long, deep breath and folded her hands across her stomach. "I wouldn't say I'm paranoid. I'm just not good at mastering my emotions. Maybe once I'm in position to take the throne, I'll feel better."

Dr. Hollands gave a confused look, then he wrote that down on his notepad. He looked at her again, but she was still staring at the ceiling. "The throne? I don't understand."

Amil took another deep breath, and out of habit, she rolled her eyes. "Are you familiar with Ivan the Terrible?"

"Not too much, very little."

"Okay listen, in 1538 his mother, Elena, died. Ivan was eight years old and became an orphan in Russia. He was supposed to be King at the time, but the boyars made fun of him because he was so small and thought that he was too young to be on the throne. It took Ivan five years to master his plan. When he turned thirteen years old, he boldly murdered the leader of the boyars and ascended to the throne. He ruled for years with an iron fist, and I must rule the same way, even if my iron fist has to be snugged inside a velvet glove."

"You're losing me, Amil. What exactly are you talking about?"

Angrily, Amil snatched the scarf from her head and pointed at it. "This is the beginning of my life. No one will ridicule me for this." She sat up, and then stood. "Because if they do, my mother will have them—"

A knock at the door interrupted her, then it came open and Falisa peeped her head inside with a smile. She came in unannounced and stood there. Amil stood motionless, staring at her mother and praying to herself that she hadn't been standing on the other side of the door listening to her.

"We must leave now," she said with a fake smile to Dr. Hollands, hoping it would be enough to keep him off balance.

Falisa hooked her arm around Amil, and she quickly tried to move toward the door to exit his office.

"Your daughter was about to tell me something that I believe may be really important. Why don't you join us?" Dr. Hollands said.

"No!" Amil said loudly "Can we just go home? I don't feel well."

Falisa spun Amil around and pointed at a poster on the wall behind them, it was an annotated picture of a brain "This is called a brain, Amil. This is what you use to think with."

While Amil was looking at the poster of the brain, Falisa made her apologies to Dr. Holland and told him that she would be in touch.

"Please be sure to schedule a follow-up session. I am concerned about Amil, and I really think that she needs further treatment."

"I will be in touch." Falisa repeated and left the office with Amil.

In the rear of the limousine, Falisa sat across from Amil with a deadly look in her eyes. She held both of Amil's hands in hers. "Look at me, Amil." she whispered. "Simple mistakes can turn into a tragedy at any given moment. Never let your right hand know what your left hand is doing. Meaning, our family business is our family business, and you never discuss it with anyone outside of our circle. Is that understood?"

Amil was looking into Falisa's eyes so hard, she could see her soul. "Yes ma'am," she whispered. "It won't happen again." She lied smoothly to her mother.

# 26

Smurf definitely respected the fact that January was in her third semester at Clark University. However, he didn't care if she would've dropped out in high school, he still was in love with her and wanted to grow with her. Smurf wasn't a ladies' man, at least he didn't think he was. He didn't have that spoken word conversation as some guys had. Therefore, he spoke very little around women unless he was comfortable with them.

With January, he felt a more solid connection. He was able to talk to her without pretending that nothing was wrong. Today, they were both in Augusta riding low key in a rental car. Falisa had forewarned them to never drive their Lamborghinis in Augusta, because the feds wouldn't hesitate to find out who the drivers were.

Smurf rode the passenger side, while January drove through Martin Luther King Boulevard. Smurf scanned the streets and avenues, knowing that it was his product that everyone was scrambling for. They had bricks for days, weeks, and months. He'd been imprisoned in South America for nearly four years, lived around other killers from all walks of life, and he made it back home to see his mother and sister again. And even more, he had made it back to January.

When she turned onto Eighth avenue, Smurf sat up in his seat. They eased up in front of a small red brick A-framed home with a chain-linked fence around the front yard. Smurf looked across January to the front of the house. An older lady peeped her head from behind the screened in front door.

He saw Six's mother and clutched the door handle. "You wanna come in with me?"

She looked at him. Her face was expressionless. "I'll sit out here. I got a few calls to make, anyway." She leaned toward Smurf and he leaned in toward her until their lips touched.

"I'll be back in a few minutes," he said and stepped out the car and walked around the rear and through the fence. When he got to the top of the steps that led to the screened in front porch, Six's mother was waiting for him with the screen door open.

Her name was Mary Livingston and she was in her late forties, and a little on the chubby side with a round face. "How you doing Miss Mary?" Smurf gave her a hug.

"I'm fine baby," she said, but her voice sounded tired and weak. She sat down on the sofa that rested on the front porch. Smurf sat next to her. She looked at him. "Why you let your hair grow like that?" she played around with his dreads.

"Really didn't have no choice. But since it's the style, I just kind of stuck with it."

Mary took a deep breath and paused to make sure she was choosing her words correctly. "Do you think you can he'p my son, Smurf? Like, with a good lawyer and stuff?"

Smurf looked at her and nodded his head. "Whatever I can do." He leaned to the side a little and reached in his pocket and pulled out a knot of money. All hundreds and fifties and peeled off six thousand dollars in cash, he folded it all together and handed it to her. "This is for you and Six, just in case you need to send him something, he can get it A.S.A.P."

"Thank you baby," she said while looking at the knot of money. She stuffed it in her apron pocket. "And what about the lawyer?"

"Let him know when he call that I'ma hire a lawyer from Atlanta to come take the case." he said, then paused. "Now I can't guarantee anything about him coming home, but I'ma make sho' I handle that for him."

"You just don't know how much I've been prayin' fo' this, baby. I'm so glad you came on home. I heard you was in prison too."

"Yes ma'am, but it wasn't in the United States. I was in South America."

She drew her head back with a confused look. "South America? How you get way over there, baby?"

Smurf smiled and his newly polished gold and diamonds sparkled in her face. "It's a long story," he said and stood up. She stood up with him, held his hand up to her mouth, and kissed the back of it. "You're a blessing, sweetheart."

Smurf gave her another hug. "I got to give you my number so he can call me." He reached in his pocket and removed a pen and wrote his number on a small piece of paper. He handed it to her and started for the front yard. He then turned around. "Let him know I got him, regardless of what."

She smiled, walked to the top of the stairs and gave him another hug. "I'm just glad, he got a real friend like you by his side."

Smurf nodded and departed from her. "Call me when he calls," he said and went back to the car where January waited for him. When he got inside, he leaned over and kissed her on the cheek.

"How did it go?" She asked and started the engine.

Smurf looked through the front windshield. "We didn't talk

about the case or nothing like that. I gave her a few dollars and left her my phone number for him to call me."

"Where are we going now?" She pulled the car out into the street. "I need to get back to Atlanta. You don't wanna see your mother and sister first before we leave?"

Smurf looked at her, glad she said that because she just reminded him about something. "Make a left right here," he told her.

January turned on Grand Boulevard and then he pointed to a white aluminum siding house. "Pull in the driveway right there."

She carefully turned into the driveway and parked behind a black Bronco. Smurf pressed the horn and the front curtain shuffled. Smurf rolled his window down and threw up his arm. No more than five minutes later, a slim guy about 5'9" came out with a duffle bag and handed it to Smurf through the window. Smurf put it between his legs and gave the guy some dap. "Everything good with you?" Smurf asked.

"Yeah, I'm good." The guy said. Then he asked. "What brings you down?"

"I just left Six mama's house. Took her some money and shit."

"You know niggas ain't respectin' that nigga. He killed a baby, brah." he said, then he added. "And they said he suppose to be snitching on some niggas too."

Smurf's eyes turned cold. "Where you hear that from? My nigga ain't snitchin'."

"That shit all in the streets."

Smurf looked at January. "Go back to his mama house." He looked back at the guy outside the car. "I'll contact you."

The guy nodded and stepped away from the car. January backed out the driveway, headed back toward Six's mother's house and parked back in the same spot. Smurf got out and walked to the front porch. Miss Mary came to the door and let him in. She had a confused look on her face. “Hey baby. What’s wrong?”

Smurf stepped onto the front porch. He didn’t want to sound too aggressive. “Do you know if Six made any statements to any detectives or anything like that?”

“If he have, he hadn’t told me anything about it, baby.”

Smurf felt a little relieved, but he needed to be sure. Six knew about murders they committed years ago, and he wasn’t leaving no loose strings untied.

“Do you mind if I wait around until he calls?”

“No baby, ya’ll come on in. I just cooked some oxtails, rice and cornbread.”

# 27

When Falisa called for Fly and Smurf to come down to Miami, she had them to come to the Fontainebleau, which was the most luxurious hotel on Miami Beach. Fly arrived by plane and brought Zoë with him. He put her up in a separate room. He was basically hiding her from Falisa because he was supposed to come alone, and was going against what she said. Fly was hard headed by twenty percent, and that twenty percent would probably lead him head on into a brick wall.

Zoë gave him everything. She knew the right words to say to him to ease his mind, and she definitely was a sex professional. That alone had Fly opened to the point where nothing else mattered. Zoë cooked breakfast every morning for him while they were in Atlanta. Some mornings, he dropped her off at school, and some mornings she wouldn't move out of bed. Drained and tired from several hours of rough sex that they'd been having since they met.

From her room, she stood in the window of the twenty first floor, overlooking the Atlantic Ocean. She was covered in a thick Fontainebleau robe with nothing on underneath, holding a glass of Bolgheri Sassicaia red wine and enjoying her view. Fly walked up behind her in an off-white linen suit, Hennessy colored Gator shoes, and a matching belt. He wrapped his hands around the small of her waist and she slowly turned around and faced him. Her beautiful eyes nearly made Fly's heart crumble.

She kissed him on his lips. "How long are you gonna be?" She asked in a sad tone of voice.

Fly cupped her round soft ass through the fabric of the robe and that made her press her body closer against his. She carefully sat her glass of wine down on the table and untied her robe. "Just five minutes. Fuck me five minutes before you leave."

Fly's mouth was all over hers. He knew he couldn't just give her five minutes. That would result in him being an entire hour late. Still, his hand found the soft wetness of her vagina lips. She grabbed for his pants in an aggressive manner.

"I wanna do something different," she whispered. She stepped closer and grinded on his fingers. "You make my pussy so wet, boo."

Fly felt his skin crawl as if a soft feather was touching him. He gripped her ass harder and pressed his body even closer to hers. "What you wanna do different?"

Zoë was sucking on his neck now, and nibbling at his earlobe. "I wanna get fucked outside on the balcony, overlooking the Atlantic Ocean."

"We might can arrange that."

DOWNSTAIRS, Falisa stood flawless in a white Dior dress and Dior heels. Pepé had arrived four hours earlier, and was standing on the outside terrace next to her. He was dressed in a suit, shirt and a stylish tie. They each held glasses of red wine.

Scarpetta was an Italian restaurant that was connected to the Fontainebleau. It was one of Pepé's favorite places to eat. The two of them toasted and looked out at the beautiful Miami scenery.

"I don't think your daughter likes me," Pepé said.

Falisa looked at him. She didn't respond, instead she turned around and looked behind her and across the terrace where Amil and Iris were sitting. Falisa gave them a smile. Iris held up her champagne glass and Falisa looked back at Pepé. "Before it's over, my daughter will love you. She's a little outspoken right now, however, she's definitely a valuable asset."

Pepé was still looking out toward the sea. "We want to double your shipment, Falisa. This is the perfect time." He paused, then continued. "We go hard one good time, then we'll vacation for eight months. What do you think?"

"You bring it. And I'll make it disappear." She sipped from her glass. "Then we'll travel the world."

She grabbed his hand and pulled him toward the table where Amil and Iris waited. Falisa sat down and Pepé sat down next to her. He felt a little uncomfortable.

He looked up and noticed Smurf and Papa Bear heading toward them.

Amil noticed too, and stood up quickly. A smile was on her face, her hair was still cut low and she wore an even tapeline. With a pair of light tinted shades on her face, she looked like a young runway model. Her legs chopped like scissors as she made her way to greet them.

Imitating Falisa's character, she got to Smurf first and gave him a brief hug. "Hey Smurf." she said happily.

"Hey Amil, how you doin'?" Smurf asked.

"I guess I'm alright," she said playfully, with a smile.

She went to Papa Bear and embraced him. She held him tight with her head pressed against his chest. "Papa," she whispered.

Amil loved Papa Bear more than she loved her late father, Timbo. The moment was quiet.

Papa Bear looked down at her. "What happened to your hair?" He rubbed his hand across her head and she smiled.

"It gets real hot in Miami, and I thought I'd try something new." She gave him a sassy look, grabbed his hand and pulled him toward the table where the rest of the family sat.

Iris stood and greeted Smurf and Papa Bear with a warm embrace, Falisa did the same. When Pepé stood up, Amil took it upon herself to be the host. "Smurf. Papa," she said. Then with a casual sway, she touched the back of Pepé's arm. "This is my stepfather, Pepé." Papa Bear shook Pepé's hand, stared him in his eyes, and slightly bowed his head.

"Nice to meet you, my friend." Pepé said in his thick Spanish accent.

"You too." Papa Bear said.

When Smurf shook his hand, he only did so briefly. He hadn't quite gotten over their past incident, and in his heart, he still carried rage about it. But out of respect for Falisa, he would keep it cool.

Pepé placed his hand on Smurf's shoulder. "You look good, my friend," Pepé said.

Amil studied both of them. Eye contact, body language, and the whole nine. She didn't know about their history. She definitely didn't know that he was the man responsible for chopping off her brother's leg.

"You too," was all Smurf said.

When they sat down, Falisa asked, "Where is Fly?"

Amil stood. "Allow me." She was ready to take off.

Falisa touched her hand. "Slow down, baby." she said. Then she looked at Smurf and gave him a nod. Smurf stood up and pulled out his cell phone.

# 28

Fly was naked, drowsy on Oxycontin pain pills, and lying in the bed clutching a bottle of Dom Perignon. He sipped straight from the bottle while Zoë lay between his legs, slowly sucking on his penis. Her seductive eyes penetrated his as she made him feel more than good. His toes curled and uncurled. The Egyptian cotton sheets were so comfortable against his skin, he was nearly about to go to sleep.

"I love this dick," she whispered and wrapped her lips and tongue around the head of his penis. When he heard his phone ring, it brought him out of his trance. *Damn! What the fuck am I doing?* He asked himself. He sat the champagne bottle on the nightstand and grabbed his cell phone.

"Talk to me." he said when he answered.

"Brah, where you at? We downstairs and you the only person missing."

Fly immediately pushed Zoë away and swung his leg out of bed. He quickly started to strap his fake on. "I'm on the way." Fly said, then added. "Give me ten minutes."

Zoë got up and sashayed into the bathroom, Fly couldn't help but to admire her body. Her ass was soft and jiggled with every step. When she faded into the bathroom, Fly hung his phone up and finished the process of snapping his leg on. He stood up naked, and began moving toward the bathroom when Zoë came back out with a steaming hot and soapy washcloth and a towel. She washed his balls and penis for him. Five minutes later, he was dressed again and out the door.

When he left, she locked the door and got on the phone. "Hey baby," she said.

FLY MET up with Smurf at the front entrance of Scarpetta and they walked to the outside terrace where everyone was. When Fly got to the table, he didn't show any feelings whatsoever toward Pepé. He walked around the table and shook everyone's hand including his mother's.

She looked at him, surprised. He never greeted her like that before, and that made her wonder. When he got to Amil, he made her stand up and he hugged her with a warm embrace. He whispered in her ear. "I love you."

She whispered back. "I love you too, Fly." She smiled up at him and kissed his cheek. She whispered in his ear again. "When I look in your eyes, I see someone else. Are you alright?"

"You're too observant, Amil." he said with a laugh. Then he found his seat and sat down and looked around the table. "So what we eating?"

"Mediterranean octopus and Key West pink shrimp," Pepé said.

Everyone looked at him with their nose turned up, except for Papa Bear. He was the only person smiling, with a look that indicated that he liked the sound of octopus and Key West pink shrimp. They chatted amongst themselves while Falisa studied Fly with slightly squinted eyes. Fly looked tired, and his eyelids were definitely becoming heavy. He was smiling and talking to Papa Bear. He cut his eyes up at Smurf as he stood up.

Smurf walked around to where Falisa was sitting and leaned down. He whispered something in her ear. She nodded, then looked around the table and smiled briefly. "Ya'll excuse me."

Nobody said a word. She stood up and walked over to the terrace. She paused, turned and faced Smurf. "What's the problem, sweetheart?"

Smurf covered his mouth with his hand, imitating the mafia guys from the movies. "I don't know for sure. But if you can, check into my old associate, Six for me."

Falisa's facial expression didn't change, and this time she covered her mouth and spoke back to him. "You don't have to say any more. Get me his full name, and I'll take it from there." she said and paused, before removing her hand from her mouth. "And for now, go ahead and enjoy yourself."

She gave him a hug and they went back to the table. There were two waiters standing around taking orders. They ordered Colorado lamb chops and Gotham steak. Iris ordered braised short ribs of beef for her and Amil. Pepé and Papa Bear ordered the Mediterranean octopus and Key West pink shrimp.

For the next two hours, they chatted with Pepé, leaving out all the hidden secrets and speaking only about fun and ways to enjoy money. Pepé shared Colombian rituals. He moved his head and eyes around the table to each one of them. Out of everyone, he still found a hidden deadly stare coming from Amil, which she tried to hide behind a phony smile.

"I can live at the Fontainebleau forever," Fly said. He casually looked around the table at their faces.

He saw Falisa staring at him. She stood up to excuse herself from the table and called Fly to come with her. He stood up with a glass of Bolgheri red wine in his hand, his face was hidden behind his dreads and he quickly moved them from his face and followed his mother over to the end of the Terrace.

She paused and turned around to face Fly. He stood about three inches taller than her, therefore she looked up into his eyes. "You alright?"

He took a sip from the glass before he responded. Then all he said was. "I'm good."

For the next five or six seconds, it seemed as if the world had gotten quiet, especially between the two of them. Fly wasn't trying to look Falisa in her eyes, but he knew he had to because that was one of their family rules.

She studied him yet again. "How's your leg feeling?" He tried smiling, but it was phony and she took a mental note of it. "The next shipment we get will be double what we got last time. Will you be ready?"

He nodded. Fly was high on Oxycontin pain pills. He couldn't see it, but Falisa definitely recognized it. Falisa grabbed Fly's face and placed her hands on each of his cheeks. She was two inches from his face.

"I can't help you if you don't want to help yourself."

"I'm good Ma," he said. "Honestly."

Falisa nodded, smiled at him, and left it at that.

## 29

A week later, Fly purchased a four-bedroom house in a gated community in North Fulton County. The house was worth a quarter of a million dollars and was a two level white brick and gray stone. This was basically a gate-way-stash house that he purchased for two reasons. One is that he wanted to have somewhere that he could keep Zoë's pretty ass at, and two, this was where he and Smurf could count their money and stash a few keys of cocaine without anyone knowing about it.

Inside the bedroom, Zoë was laying naked on nearly three hundred thousand dollars in cash. Fly sat at the foot of the bed with a set of crutches leaning next to him. He was counting casually, and once he finished a thousand, he'd hand it over to Zoë to rubber band it and drop it in a huge Foot Locker bag.

Zoë looked at Fly. "I found some new pain pills baby, they have a bitch floatin'." She snuggled up against him. "And they make my pussy so damn wet."

Fly laughed, but never responded. Instead, he continued to count by hand. Then he just threw a handful of money in the air and watched it slowly trickle to the floor and bed. When he lay back, he propped his hands behind his head.

"You already got a nigga bout to OD on that good ass pussy between yo' legs."

She laughed and lay up close to him and began rubbing her hands across his chest. Then she nibbled on his earlobe, and began to slowly suck on his neck. Fly closed his eyes. It was as if she'd had some kind of hypnotic effect on him. An effect that made him relax and rest. She put her mouth on his, and he immediately removed his hands from behind his head and ran his fingers through her hair. He slowly caressed her thin face.

Tonight, Zoë wore earth tone eye shadow, and that made her sex appeal raise another notch. Fly cupped her breasts and began sucking on her rose-red nipples, going from one to the other. Zoë began making erotic sounds with her mouth, and even purring like a cat. She slowly licked his chest, making an invisible line with her tongue all the way down to his navel. The closer she got to his growing member, the harder his chest and stomach rose and fell. Zoë massaged him and worked her way down to the head of his penis. She slowly wrapped her mouth around it as if she was toying around with a chocolate blow pop. Fly took a deep breath, her mouth and wet tongue felt so good that he clutched a hand full of the satin sheets that were on the bed.

"Just relax, baby," she whispered. Then she deep throated him.

He frowned, and it felt so good that he carefully placed his hand on the back of her head. One hundred dollar bills were sticking to her back and ass cheeks. When Fly pulled her up, she straddled him and eased his long dark piece of meat into her fat, bald vagina. She eased down on him, stretching her walls. Fly opened his mouth, just slightly though as if he was gasping for air. When she rotated her wide hips and placed her hands in the center of his chest, he could do nothing but close his eyes and relax.

He was turned out on the high-powered pain pills, and was taking up to six or seven a day. For the next two hours, Zoë milked him and fucked him to sleep. They were both high on the pills and covered in dried cum and sweat. When she eased out the bed, Fly's eyes popped open. He quietly watched her go to her Gucci handbag and remove a small plastic bag. Her back was to Fly, but she was peeping at him through the mirror while standing naked at the dresser.

When she finally opened the small sack of her powder substance, she dipped her nail down in the bag, brought it up to her nostril, and sniffed. She frowned and made a funny sound as if it stung.

"What you sniffing?" Fly asked, then he sat up.

Zoë tried to drop the bag back in her handbag, as if he'd startled her. She turned and faced him, then walked back toward him and stood directly in front of him. Fly put his hands around her waist and began to firmly massage her soft ass cheeks. "Just a lil coke, baby."

Fly grunted, but he didn't say anything. She dropped her arms around his neck. "You got my pussy sore, boo."

She inched up close to his face and he began to suck on her clit and finger her at the same time. She pushed his head away and stepped back playfully with a smile on her face. "I wanna get in the Jacuzzi and relax. Then I wanna fix some drinks and feed you fruit and suck your long chocolate dick for the rest of the night."

"Sounds like a plan, baby," he whispered.

She picked up Fly's crutches from the floor and gave them to him. He stood up and headed toward the bathroom. She watched him go inside, and she went underneath his pillow and grabbed his gun and put it in her Gucci bag. She left the bedroom, walked into the kitchen, and picked up the phone to call her boyfriend and his crew. This was a planned robbery, which was sweet as taking candy from a baby. The line rang six times and went to his voicemail.

She knew he had his phone. Maybe he didn't recognize the number. She went back into the bedroom and heard the water running in the Jacuzzi. She grabbed her bag and got her cell phone. All she had to do was get him on the phone, leave the house, and let them in. When she stepped into a pair of jeans she punched his cell number while walking through the house and out into the garage. The phone rang and rang, and still no answer.

The cocaine had her paranoid. She stepped out into the cold garage, unlocked the side door, and poked her head out, but nobody was there. Her heart began thumping rapidly inside of her chest as worry spread through her body. *Where the fuck y'all at?* She wondered.

She hung up and redialed again. When she didn't get an answer, she realized that something was terribly wrong. Zoë went back inside the house and stripped herself naked again. She couldn't let him see her dressed, because he would know something was up and out of place. Damn! They were supposed to be parked out front. Her stomach was flipping in knots now.

"Zoë." Fly called out.

With a stir of nervousness, she yelled back. "I'm fixing the drinks, Boo." She went to the kitchen and quickly poured two glasses of Hennessy.

Her heart was thumping even harder now, and she spilled Hennessy on the marble countertop.

# 30

When she got back into the bedroom, she threw her pants in the corner and walked into the bathroom where Fly was soaking in the bubbled water. The walls were lined with mirrors.

Zoë looked at her own reflection and saw the panicky look in her eyes, and desperately tried to make it disappear. She sat on the edge of the Jacuzzi and handed him the glass of Hennessy.

Her phone rang from the bedroom. She stood up. "I'll be right back," she said.

She went back into the bedroom, knowing that this was him. It was definitely time. Money was scattered all over the floor and bed. *Lord, this is it,* she said to herself.

When she picked up the phone, she saw that it was indeed her boyfriend's number splashed across the screen. She breathed easier now. "Hey Boo. Where ya'll at?"

"Right plan sweetheart, just the wrong man." A soft and elegant voice said from the other end.

Zoë stopped breathing for a second. Then in a lower tone of voice, she asked, "Who is this?"

"My name is Falisa," she said from the other end. "I'm Fly's mother, okay? Now, don't panic and try to leave the house. You can go ahead and lock the door back because your people won't be visiting tonight." She paused. "Go ahead and secure the door."

Zoë was so nervous she was nearly about to have a break down. She walked through the house naked, and still with the phone pressed against the side of her face. When she got to the garage, she quickly locked the door and spoke back into the phone. "It's locked." Her voice trembled. She looked around the garage in a panicked stare.

"Good, here's the deal. I want you to go back to your regular scheduled program and enjoy yourself with my son. Don't tell him anything, you understand? Can you keep a secret?"

"Yes. I understand." She went back inside the house and locked the door to the utility closet. Her eyes had turned moist. "What about my boyfriend?" she asked.

"I asked you can you keep a secret, and you asked me about your boyfriend." Falisa's voice was calm and steady. Then she responded. "Everyone is alright. Get a good night's rest. Tomorrow at eleven am sharp, you'll meet me at Phipps Plaza for lunch. Don't disrespect me by doing anything other than what I say."

Zoë swallowed. "Yes ma'am. I'll be there, I promise."

"So once again. Can you keep a secret?"

"Yes ma'am, I can." Her hands were shaking like an out of line car axle.

The line went dead.

Zoë was shook, and it showed all over her face. Her heart raced inside her chest, pumping more fear with every beat. She went to the bathroom and heard Fly singing a verse from 2 Pac's song, "Dear Momma".

"When I was young, me and Mama had beef, seventeen years old kicked out on the streets. Though back in the times, I thought I'd neva see her face, ain't a woman alive that can take my mama place."

When Zoë heard him sing that verse, her stomach felt nauseated. Then she called out. "Boo?"

"Damn girl. It's taking you long enough."

She began to walk toward the bathroom. Fly was sitting in the Jacuzzi. He smiled when he saw her. "Come on in, the water feels good."

She tried to give him a smile, but it was weak. She stepped in the water, his crutches fell behind her and she nearly jumped out of her skin. Fly had to brace her. "Damn! You scared like that?"

She sat down in the water and kissed him. In the back of her mind, she was in fear for her life.

AT 10:45 the following morning, Zoë was on the phone with Falisa and walking though Phipps Plaza on the Nordstrom wing. When she got in front of the Bally's store, Falisa appeared in her eyesight. "You see me?" Falisa asked through the phone.

Zoë was nervous. She was looking Falisa dead in her face. Iris stood in the store and watched both of them through the glass.

Falisa extended her hand out to Zoë. She shook it. "How's my daughter-in-law feeling this morning?"

Zoë didn't really know how to respond. She swallowed and fear jumped in her eyes, along with tears. "I don't know what to say, Miss Falisa."

"For one, drop the miss and call me Falisa. Two, you need to get yourself together. You look like you've seen a ghost. Trust me sweetheart, if I wanted to hurt you, it would've happened last night." She placed her hand on Zoë's shoulder. "Let's go in here. You got time to do some shopping?"

Zoë took a deep breath, and then she nodded her head. Falisa turned and led Zoë inside the Bally store. Zoë looked Falisa up and down and couldn't help but to admire her nicely shaped body and how she walked in her Christian Louboutin *Bianca* pumps and two-piece pant suit.

Inside the store, Falisa looked at men's shoes. She looked at Zoë. "You think Fly will like these?"

Zoë's stomach tightened a little. She could barely speak. "No offense Miss Falisa, but I'm scared. I can't even think straight."

Falisa smiled and patted her hand. "That's understandable. Come on, walk with me." Falisa walked to the left side of the store where leather bags for men hung on the wall. She paused and looked at the bags, and then she began asking a couple of questions. "First, I need a damn good answer as to why you wanted to rob my son." Falisa removed a soft leather Bally bag from the wall, and never looked in Zoë's direction.

"It's just my routine hustle, Miss Falisa. I didn't—"

"Routine hustle?" Falisa said calm and coolly. She held up the bag and eyed the manager. She was letting him know that she wanted it, and never mind the price. "I was under the impression that you were a student at Spelman."

Zoë got quiet.

"You better speak, sweetheart, cause a closed mouth don't get fed." She still wasn't looking at Zoë. Falisa went down the row to another leather bag. She removed it from the hook and held it up.

"I'm not in school. I just was tryin' to help my people out."

"Where you from?"

"I'm from here. Atlanta."

"Where do my son think you from?"

"Missouri."

"The show me state," Falisa smiled. When she finally looked at her, her eyes were cold as ice. "So you're not at Spelman, and you're not from Missouri, and I'm assuming since you were trying to have my son robbed, that you're not in love with him either."

First Zoë's eyes went to the floor, and then she lowered her head. Falisa placed her finger underneath her chin and raised her head.

"The only reason I respect your hustle is because you're a woman. However, the brief description I'll give you of myself is something like the Bermuda Triangle. You know it's a no fly zone, right?"

Zoë looked at her with a confused look across her face. "I've heard the myths and stuff about it."

"Well, what I'm trying to say is, you would have a better chance of crossing the Bermuda Triangle, than crossing me or anybody that's in my family."

Iris approached them from the rear, dressed the same as Falisa in her two-piece pant suit and Christian Louboutins. Without saying anything to Zoë, she went to Falisa and whispered, "Lunch at the Tavern."

Falisa nodded, then she looked at Zoë. "Come on sweetheart, we're going to lunch."

At the Tavern, Falisa, Zoë, and Iris had a reserved table where they ate Asian lettuce wraps filled with satay chicken, crunchy Chinese vegetables and water chestnuts.

"You're young and very attractive, Zoë. At least you used your real name. But I'll be straight forward with you. If Fly ever finds out about this..." She paused and looked around to confirm that no one was in earshot. She leaned in closer toward her. "He will kill you, okay?"

Fear jumped back into her eyes, but she still managed to nod her head.

"But don't worry, sweetheart. Tomorrow you'll enroll at Spelman, expenses on me. If you're not in love with my son, from today forward, you are. And, if you're wondering about your boyfriend, that's something you're just gonna have to get out your head okay."

"Why?"

Falisa bit into her wrap and looked at Iris as if she was telling her to share the news. Iris looked at Zoë and said. "They're gone to Missouri," she said coldly, and then she added, "In pieces."

Falisa checked her watch. She had a meeting to go to in Miami. She stood up and gave Zoë a hand to shake. Zoë shook her hand while looking up at her. "You leaving? I thought we were shopping."

Falisa smiled at Zoë. "Honey, I just rewarded you with the greatest gift that money could buy, and that's your life."

Iris stood up, then her and Falisa hugged. "Make sure all her paper work for Spelman is officially ready." She kissed Iris' cheek and then departed.

# 31

Pepé was camera shy. Falisa on the other hand, was camera ready every time she stepped out in public. Over the last eight weeks, Falisa and Pepé had gone on tour across the United States. They spent a week in Augusta and caught the Masters Golf Tournament, and she had finally gotten the chance to meet Tiger Woods in person. They'd flown to Dallas, Texas, just to donate thirty thousand to a charity fund; they danced at the ball together and rubbed shoulders with politicians in that region.

When they got back to Florida, Pepé wanted to do something he hadn't done since Falisa was in Chia with him. They leased a helicopter and had the pilot to fly them from Miami up to South Carolina to the Aiken Polo Club. They'd made special reservations for them to land on the concrete landing pad on the property of Whitney Field. When they arrived, they were both dressed in jeans and Polo riding boots and Polo shirts. One of the members of the club escorted them to a private seating area. It was basically, a VIP section where they could sit and enjoy a nice game of polo.

The weather was nice and sunny on that Sunday afternoon.

They were escorted to their table and were surrounded by other couples and families that had come out to enjoy themselves as well. Pepé carried a leather Polo bag on his shoulder. He sat down and removed the bag, unzipped it, and pulled out his own cigars and alcohol along with a pair of mini binoculars for Falisa. She picked them up and looked out across the three hundred yard, full sized field.

In the game of polo, you only have four players on a team, and each player's jersey number indicated the position he or she was playing. The man with the #1 on his jersey plays the forward position and the #4 player always plays the back. Then you have #2 and #3 who play the partial roles in the game. Falisa didn't know anything about the two teams that were playing each other, but she rooted for the team that wore the black and white jerseys. Watching them race from one end to the other on strong muscular horses was exciting to her. The players battled each other with long handle mullets that were wrapped with rubber grips. She allowed her eyes to prowl around. There was a rich white couple to the left of her who watched the game without allowing anything to distract them.

Falisa looked at Pepé while he relaxed and smoked his cigars and studied the game from behind a pair of tinted shades. Falisa reached underneath the table and rubbed his thigh. He turned toward her as her hand began to massage his penis through his jeans; it was growing and running half way to his kneecap. She gripped and squeezed until he became harder and harder. Then, she snuggled up against him, playing her position as a millionaire's wife the best way she knew how.

Manipulation.

"I wanna ride," she whispered.

Pepé blew out a line of smoke, flipped up his shades, and gave her a devious grin. "Si, I'm ready for you too."

"No silly, I'm talking about riding the polo horse." she said, then she kissed his neck. "And after the horse ride, I'll ride your dick, Pepé."

Pepé looked at her, his eyes were opaque and half closed. He leaned in and kissed her mouth softly. She slid her tongue into his mouth. They were lost in each other for a brief moment until the black and white polo team scored a point and everyone around them began cheering and clapping.

Falisa broke her kiss to see what all the commotion was about. When she saw that her team had scored, she began to clap also. She turned toward Pepé, he was smoking his cigar, twirling it in his mouth. He stood up and looked around until his eyes found one of the assistants for the Polo Club. Pepé waved him over. The assistant was a well-groomed white guy who was handsomely dressed.

Pepé walked with him, away from the lounge section where he and Falisa were sitting. He extended his hand out to the club assistant. They shook hands briefly, then Pepé asked him in his broken English, "My wife... would like to ride. Can you arrange?"

The assistant gave him a look that would physically apologize to him. "I'm sorry sir, but it's against the Polo Club rules and policy to ride on Sunday."

"I'm a club member."

"And I understand that, sir. But if I authorize that, I could lose my job."

Frustrated, Pepé turned away from him and waved his hand dismissively. He walked away from the guy while still smoking his cigar, leaving trails of smoke as he went back to the lounge section where Falisa was waiting and sipping on a glass of fresh lemonade through a straw. Her eyes flashed up at him. His look told her that something didn't go as planned.

Pepé sat down next to her and began mumbling Spanish curse words and watching the game. He was angry now, far more than he was just five minutes ago. Inside his leather bag was his cell phone. He removed it, then he punched in a phone number, but the call didn't go through because an incoming call came in first. Pepé answered the call. It was his brother Carlos on the other end.

They spoke back and forth in Spanish for five minutes, and then he hung up and looked at Falisa. "The name you gave me. The Livingston guy, he no good. He's turned."

Falisa's face went slack and she stared at Pepé for about twenty seconds. She reached in her bag and pulled out another cell phone and dialed one number. Papa Bear answered on the second ring.

"Hello."

"Hey, Papa." That was all she said before hanging up.

Pepé stood up again. "Come on, we go to Argentina. I buy your own polo team," he said arrogantly.

# 32

It was the summer of '97, and the Augusta heat was blazing with blinding sunrays. However, on the sixth floor of 401 Walton Way, the weather felt cold. At least that's how Anthony 'Six' Livingston felt, standing 6'4" and clad in his two-piece dark blue uniform that was issued by the Richmond County jail. Six was experiencing a lot of pressure right now, and he didn't know how to handle it. His basketball career had gone down the drain. He had once envisioned himself as an NBA first round draft pick, now all he wanted was his freedom.

After Fly and Smurf took their trip to Miami and wound up in a South American prison, Six had separated from the family. Since nineteen ninety-three, he'd completed high school and continued to grow his relationship with Jewel. She was there at every game, and made sure that he graduated from high school. Then he went off to college, Georgia Tech at that, where he was a great addition to their basketball team.

Jewel never left Augusta, and had gone to Paine College. Angel went into the Navy. Six found himself back home damn near every weekend, just to see Jewel, until she came up pregnant. Six started to lose focus on his basketball career. Jewel had gotten fat after she had their son, and Six was totally turned off by her physical appearance and her nagging behavior.

Six turned to cocaine and heavy alcohol. Then one afternoon, he was alone in the apartment, watching their five-month-old son, while Jewel went to a doctor appointment. Their baby was crying while Six was trying to flirt with a female neighbor that stayed in the complex. When he walked into the living room, the baby was crying uncontrollably in the bed.

Six picked up his son's fragile body and growled. "Shut the fuck up," he yelled, but not loud enough that the girl outside could hear him. Then he shook his son two quick times, not realizing his power was too much for the infant. The baby grew quiet within seconds.

He put the baby back in the baby bed, and went back outside to finish his conversation with the female. He didn't realize that he'd broken his own son's neck. That was over a year ago, and he'd been in the county jail awaiting trial, since then. The situation he was in wasn't looking good. The first deal they brought to him was to plea out to life without parole, or lose in trial and get the death penalty. He decided not to take either one, and give the state and feds some information about a couple of murders that he knew about. One was the incident at the University Hospital with himself, Smurf and Fly.

His mind was made up. He wasn't going to prison at all, and that was that. As he stared from his cell window down into the front parking lot six floors below, he saw his mother stepping down from the passenger side of her car. He smiled. It was time for visitation. He turned and went to the mirror to check himself and make sure his appearance was up to par. It occurred to him that his mother had gotten out on the passenger side of her car instead of the driver's side. He turned and went back to the window and looked down to the parking lot in time to see the driver side door open.

Six squinted his eyes to make sure they weren't playing a trick on him. *I must be dreaming.* he thought. He stared harder, because the man that had stepped from the driver side of the Eddie Bauer SUV was none other than Papa Bear. He leaned against the hood, crossed his feet, and pulled out his harmonica. He raised his head and bowed it. Six's heart plunged into the pit of his stomach. He took a deep breath, and as he moved away from the window, he knew why Papa Bear was with his mother. He paced the floor, realizing that something was terribly wrong.

He went back to the window and looked down. Papa Bear was still there, playing his harmonica. Six knew his signature, and that made a chill run through his veins like no other.

When Six's government name was called across the PA system, his Adam's apple bobbed in his throat. He tried to make himself relax by taking deep breaths, but for some reason, it wasn't working. He finally stepped out of his one-man cell to walk across the dorm floor. He felt his legs wobble a little. Through the Sally port, the officer upstairs in the booth buzzed him through the door, and he walked out into the corridor and made his way to the visitation area where a row of seats were on each side. A glass partition separated the visitor from the inmate. Six went to the third booth, where his mother was waiting. He picked up the phone from his side, and she picked it up from her side.

Staring each other in the eye, he tried to give her a smile. Just when his mouth curled, her eyes turned teary and she began to cry. A desperate, worried look masked her face.

"Hey Mama. What's wrong?" Six said. "What is Papa Bear doin' down there?"

His mother still didn't respond. Her stare penetrated his eyes. She was giving off so much pain that it spilled right into

Six's soul. She slowly raised her hand and placed it flat on the glass. Six pressed his hand on the glass, also as if they were touching.

Her voice cracked through the phone. "Six, what did you do, baby?"

His heart tightened inside his chest. He figured that they knew that he had flipped. "I'm trying to come home, Mama."

Her eyes dropped down and she wiped them with the back of her hand. She spoke softly into the phone. "Baby, Smurf was gonna get you a lawyer and everything. You gave him your word on the phone." She paused and shook her head, desperately trying to find the right words to deliver to her son. "Now he's at my house wit' yo' grandmama."

"For what?" Six shouted.

"What did you do, Six?" her voice was low and sad.

He didn't respond; he could only shake his head. His mother dropped her head and broke down in tears to the point that a sheriff came out and brought her some paper towels. She faked a smile at the officer and wiped her face. When he walked off, she built herself back up and took a deep breath.

She looked Six dead in his eyes. "He said... He say... if they don't read about you in tomorrow's newspaper..." She paused and sniffed. "That you was gonna read about me and yo' grandmama."

Six couldn't believe what he was hearing. How did they find out? He thought about telling the police to save his mother, but damn what about grandma? Six dropped the phone and it fell, hanging by the metal cord. He put his elbows on his knees and buried his face in pure disgust. He wasn't prepared for this. He didn't think Smurf would calculate such a strategic move.

"Just tell the police you lied, baby. Take yo' statement back."

Six ignored her. He knew it wasn't that easy.

"If you got to go to prison, I'll visit every week, baby. I don't wanna visit your grave."

Six finally looked up at his mother, staring through fiery red-veined eyes. When he looked at her, he saw Smurf, and thought about Papa Bear downstairs in the parking lot. He knew their M.O., and the caliber of Smurf and Papa Bear.

He finally stood up like a soldier, cradled the phone, and stared into his mother's eyes one last time. "I love you Mama. Tell gran'ma I love her also, okay?" That was all he could say and he really meant it. Then he walked away from her without another word.

When Six got back into his cell, he locked himself in. He went to the window and looked down. Papa Bear was still standing there at the front of the Explorer. He took a deep breath. Six fell to his knees in the middle of the floor and locked his fingers together in a prayer position.

"God, please help me," he closed his eyes and said. "Please don't let nothing happen to my family."

His chest was burning, rising and falling. Tears streaked his face and he prayed until there was nothing left inside of him. He finally broke all the way down and sobbed like a child.

The following morning, Six was all over the Channel 12 news and the front page of the Augusta Chronicle. The former Josey High School basketball player, Anthony 'Six' Livingston from Augusta was found dead late last night, hanging from a sheet in an apparent suicide.

# 33

Time was moving fast, and Falisa was definitely trying her best to make sure that every thread was sewn in tight, and definitely all loose ends were snipped. The last shipment of cocaine was in her possession. Nearly two tons, and she made it do what it was supposed to do. With her husband, Pepé, having a couple of DEA agents on his payroll, there was no way that she could go wrong. She made sure that Fly was doing his part, and had Zoë as his guardian angel. Her life was still on the line, and she would never even think about crossing Fly again.

In the last three months, Pepé and Falisa had bought their own team, and Falisa had purchased a set of personal riding horses for herself, Amil, and Iris. Her polo team was in Florida, and her trainer was making sure that her investment was good, so she put that in the back of her mind.

Today, she was at Papa Bear's farm, where she'd had a state of the art horse barn built. It had a concrete floor, rustproof steel walls, garage bays and twelve galvanized steel horse stalls that were fifty-one inches wide, seven feet high, and equipped with central air and heat. This was also another way of sealing

Timbo's body in concrete underground. The entire facility cost her one point five million, and that's not including the horses. It was four o'clock in the evening when Falisa, Iris and Amil entered the barn.

Papa Bear was already inside and waiting. He'd settled their horses for them. The first one he removed from the stall was Falisa's. Her horse was all-white with bright eyes the size of apples. Carefully, he pulled him by his reigns outside where his horseshoes click clacked against the concrete. Falisa rubbed his coat, and only addressed him as 'Beautiful'.

She climbed on him and secured her feet. "I'll be out front," she said.

She pulled the leather rein and her and beautiful trotted slowly out front. Papa Bear removed Amil's horse next. Hers was all-black with a glossy, wet looking coat, but her saddle was white, and that stood out.

Before Papa Bear handed her the reins, he placed his hand on her shoulder and looked her in her eyes. "Do I have to tell you to be careful?"

She shook her head with a smile. "You know I'm an excellent rider."

Papa Bear gave her the leather reins and she bounced up on the horse's back like a professional. She looked down at Iris. "I'll wait on you," she told her.

Iris moved her horse from the stall herself. Papa Bear allowed it, only because he knew that Iris knew what she was doing. Iris climbed up on her brown horse and made him turn around in a circle, then she and Amil walked out on their horses side by side.

When they all were outside the barn, Falisa tapped the horse with her right foot and made the horse take off running through the riding trail. Falisa had taken riding lessons a couple of weeks ago, along with Iris and Amil, so they were all very familiar with it. Falisa stopped and turned around. She and her horse waited for Iris and Amil as the horse kicked up dust.

"You can't ride casual every time," she yelled at them as they slowly approached.

"Stop being a show off, Mother," Amil said. She was getting closer to Falisa, and now the three of them fell in step together. They moved along the path through the trees where the sun shined on them from different angles, because the trees were blocking most of it.

Iris looked over at Falisa. "Now this is the life."

Falisa smiled. "You damn right, this is definitely good living. This is what the ending of a good movie should end be. No stress. Nothing to worry about. We got long money."

"I can't tell," Amil said. "I asked you to get me a pink Ferrari so I can represent breast cancer awareness."

"Ferraris do not come in pink, Amil, and you don't know how to drive a stick yet. I think you'll look better in a Porsche, anyway. Who knows? The sweet sixteenth birthday is coming up for you."

Amil looked at Falisa and made her horse pick up his pace and move in front of her. She blocked Falisa, and all three of them stopped.

Falisa smiled at Amil. "What?" She asked with a touch of laughter in her voice.

"I'm ready to walk in your shoes, Mother. For sure, after I turn sixteen."

Falisa could do nothing but continue her smile. "Then if you get angry, Amil, and you're in position, how do I know you won't self-destruct?"

"How do you know Fly won't self-destruct either?"

"Rome wasn't built in a day, baby. This is our family empire, and with me, I'll make the final—"

Just then, an Eastern Diamondback rattlesnake slithered out of nowhere and struck the leg of Falisa's horse. The horse yelped and bucked wildly and out of control. Falisa's eyes widened with fear. The horse flipped her off his back as if she was a piece of paper.

She went in the air and landed awkwardly on her back. Her neck cracked as she crashed to the ground. The wild horse bucked again and his rear hoofs crushed her rib cage. Falisa yelled out in pain.

Immediately, Iris removed her Glock and put two slugs in the horse's head before he did any more damage. Iris hopped down from her horse and looked at Amil. "Go get Papa, and tell him to call an ambulance."

Without a word, Amil took off on her horse and raced toward the barn. Papa Bear was already running towards her with a mini assault rifle, his eyes were wide as he nearly aimed the weapon at her. Amil slowed down her horse. She had a panicked look in her eyes and nervousness running through her veins. Her own breath was coming in quick pants. Her stare was dead on Papa Bear.

"She fell off the horse, Papa." She pulled on the reigns of her horse to slow him down. She had the horse spinning in circles, but kept her eyes on him.

Papa Bear's eyes widened. He pointed toward the house. "Go call the ambulance," he yelled at her.

Without a word, Amil took off on the horse and dust kicked up as she went. Papa Bear began pumping his legs and running as fast as he could. All he knew was that some shots were fired, and the assault rifle was running with him. When he emerged from the trees and bushes, he saw Iris cradling Falisa's head while she was lay motionless on the ground.

The horse was lying flat on his side, no more than two feet away, and the flies were already beginning to swarm around the mouth, nose and bullet wounds. When Papa Bear reached Iris and Falisa, it felt as if his heart would jump out of his chest. Her body was twisted in an abnormal position, her ribcage was crushed, and she was spitting up blood. Her chest was rising and falling very quickly and a blood bubble formed from her mouth.

Papa Bear fell to his knees next to her. He was about to touch her, when Iris held up a hand to stop him.

"We can't wait on no ambulance," Papa Bear said.

"We can't move her. Her neck maybe broken," Iris managed to say. Her tears forced their way from the back of her eyes and pushed out until one rolled down Iris' cheek.

Papa Bear knew Falisa had a punctured lung or some type of internal bleeding going on. When he kissed her forehead, he whispered, "You better hold on."

He stood to his feet and took off running, leaving his assault rifle behind. He wasn't waiting on the ambulance, he was going to get the SUV.

# 34

Two hours later, the majority of the family was in the waiting room of the prestigious Doctor's Hospital on Wheeler road. After she finally arrived and the doctors took her into surgery, she had three severe seizures and slipped into a deep coma. Iris, Amil, and Papa Bear were there from the beginning. Smurf and January arrived next. Fly and Zoë came together.

Fly was walking with an all-white cane, and he had a very depressed look on his face. He saw Amil leaning against Papa Bear, and he had his arm wrapped around her. He figured she was on the verge of breaking down again. Shades covered his eyes, and his dreads were all over his head. They had their own private family waiting room, and Fly looked around at everyone to see if their emotions and tears were authentic.

Iris sat in a cushioned chair all alone and staring down towards the floor, lost in her own thoughts. When she raised her head, Fly noticed how puffy and swollen her eyes were. She looked at Fly. They shared the exact same pain and grief. Her heart was aching so much for Falisa, she'd gone through too much for it to end like this. With her eyes open, and still staring at Fly, she said a silent prayer for Falisa and the rest of the family.

Fly walked across the room and tapped Amil on her arm. She looked up at him through glossy, wet eyes. “Come here.”

She stood up, and Fly exited the private waiting room and walked out into the corridor with Amil next to him. He eased his arm around her neck. “You alright?”

She nodded her head and said. “Yes.”

There was a small room to their left that was occupied with vending machines filled with sandwiches, soda, and chips. When they walked inside, the room was empty. Fly held both of Amil hands and stopped in front of her so they were looking each other square in the eye. He removed his shades and hung them on the neck of his shirt.

“If anything happens to Mama, we’ll keep her alive through us. As of now, I’m the head of the family and I’ll make sure everything still runs like it should.”

“Are you serious, Fly? I mean really, do you think you can fill Mother’s shoes?”

“I’m not tryin’ to fill her shoes, Amil. I’m only making sure you’re alright, the money is alright, and all other business.”

Amil didn’t respond. She just looked at him and slowly shook her head, while saying to herself, *you just don’t understand*.

“You looking at me like it’s a problem or something.”

“It is. For one, I really don’t think you’re capable of handling big money and making wise decisions, Fly.”

Fly let out a soft, cold, mirthless laugh. “You’ve really turned into someone else.” He shook his head and let her hands go. He moved his face close to hers, and spoke in a light angry tone of voice. “You’re my little sister, Amil, and I love you to death. Okay? To death, bottom line.”

She stood in silence for a moment, looking up at Fly as he

backed away from her. When he turned his back to leave, she coldly spoke. "If you love me, why would you leave that dude Ox alive, after you know he kidnapped me?"

He faced her he gave a twisted look as if he couldn't believe what his ears were hearing. She wasn't supposed to know anything about that, he didn't know where she got the information, and surely didn't want to give her the wrong response. "So you want him dead?"

Her head slowly moved up and down, as if she was unsure. That was her outer expression. In her heart, she was ready to glorify the demise of him, and anyone else who was responsible.

Without warning, Fly dropped his cane to the floor and tightly gripped Amil just below her shoulders. He roughly pulled her to him. When she jerked toward him, her eyes were stretched wide with fear.

He growled in a low tone. "Understand this, baby sistah. United we stand, divided we'll fall. We'll never argue amongst each other. Our bond is like no other, since we were babies. What's going on with you?" His voice was turning into a mere whisper, then he went on. "Our mother is here on her death bed, where do you get room for these other issues?" He released her arms and hugged her tight. He kissed the top of her head. "I love you, baby sistah."

Her arms wrapped around his waist and she cried on his chest. Her words came between sobs. "I... don't want... nothing... to happen... to Mother."

Fly held onto her for nearly five minutes until a white coated doctor appeared in the doorway. "Excuse me, sir."

Fly looked up at him. His stare was cold as ice, then he caught himself. "Yeah?"

"Come with me, please," he said and walked out into the corridor.

Fly and Amil followed him. They both felt like they were

walking toward a death trap. Papa Bear appeared from the other waiting room and fell in step with them. The doctor led them toward a door with the three bold letters ICU on it. When he pushed the door open, Falisa was across the room on her bed with two nurses and two other doctors standing over her.

They stopped, then the doctor faced them. "The surgery was successful. She has three broken ribs and a punctured lung, which is what caused the internal bleeding."

"Is she still in a coma?" Papa Bear asked him, with deep concern in his voice.

"Unfortunately, yes she is. But she's well taken care of. We'll be sending her to MCG where the certified trauma unit is. No doubt, she's a fighter. Her husband is due in tonight, and is bringing his own neurologist in to consult with our staff."

Amil looked up at the doctor. "Can I see her?"

The doctor didn't want to refuse her, however his eyes shifted to Papa Bear since he was the adult. "Due to her condition, I wouldn't recommend it. But with your consent..."

Papa Bear turned toward Amil. Her eyes were moist, but Papa knew she was tough. He grabbed her hands and pulled her to the side, away from Fly and the doctor. With his eyes boring into hers, he asked, "You wanna see her?"

A tear rolled down her cheek and Papa wiped it away with his thumb. Her head moved up and down. Amil's heart was rumbling inside of her chest. Papa Bear smiled, something that he didn't do too often.

He turned back toward the doctor and Fly. "We wanna see her."

The doctor smiled, bowed his head, and turned toward the hospital bed where Falisa was. He walked in that direction and they followed close behind him. When they finally got close to Falisa, the doctors opened a small space. It looked as if Falisa was trapped inside a spider web. The machine that breathed for her sounded like a loud animal.

Amil turned away, and buried her face in Papa Bear's chest. Fly recognized his little sister's acting skills, but he would keep quiet until he felt that the timing was right. The important thing now, was their mother. He would do anything to aid in her recovery. He would even tolerate Pepé for the time being.

# 35

Four days later, Falisa was transferred to the Medical College of Georgia, still in a coma. Amil was there with her, along with Iris. They both sat patiently, beside her hospital bed. Amil cared for her the most, brushing her hair and washing her face, and sometimes even holding a full conversation with Falisa as if she was responding to her questions. Iris sat in a corner chair with reading glasses on her face and scanning a USA Today newspaper.

Amil was close to Falisa's ear, whispering again. "So you just gonna ignore me, Mother?"

Falisa's eyes were closed. A fat plastic tube emerged from inside her mouth, and hooked up to several machines that kept her alive. When Iris cut her eyes at Amil, she saw her wiping the side of Falisa's face and forehead with a damp cloth.

"I'll make sure the family is well taken care of, Iris is here with me. Fly and Smurf are handling all the necessary legwork. Well, I don't have to tell you about Papa, you definitely know he's on top of everything. But it's no fun without you. No one can keep the party live like you, Mother." Amil took a deep breath, paused for a second or two, and went on. "But I'll hold you down until you come back, okay?"

A soft knock came from the door, and Iris and Amil turned their heads toward it as it opened. Fly stepped in, with Zoë behind him. They brought in balloons, flowers, and two boxes of Pizza Hut pizza. Iris stood up, and dropped her newspaper in the chair. She smiled and hugged Fly, and then out of respect, she gave Zoë a hug also.

"How she doing?" Zoë asked Iris, then she sat the two boxes of pizza down.

"She still the same."

Fly walked over to Amil and gave her a hug. While hugging him, she rolled her eyes at Zoë, but Zoë didn't catch it. "How you feeling?" Fly asked Amil.

"I'm fine." she said. "What about you?"

"I'm good." he whispered, then separated from her and looked down at his mother.

He touched the side of her face, and then leaned down and kissed her cheek. He could barely stand to see her in this helpless position. Fly sat down next to her in the chair where Amil had sat.

He leaned in close to her and whispered, "Hey beautiful. I just stopped by to let you know that everything is under control." He paused and took a deep breath to grab a hold of himself. "I'm about to do something that you probably wouldn't approve of, and I'ma apologize for it ahead of time." He kissed her forehead and stood up.

He looked over at Iris. "I'm taking Amil with me for a couple hours."

"Where we going?" Amil asked.

Fly placed a finger on his lips. "Shhh," he said. "It's a secret." He looked at Zoë and motioned for her to come closer. When she did, he put his arm around her neck and kissed her. "Stay with Iris until I get back."

A sad look crossed her face. "Where you going, Fly?"

"Family business, baby. Just do what I say."

Without another word, he left the hospital room with Amil.

FLY RODE in the backseat of a Yukon, Amil sat next to him, and an older guy was driving. Fly didn't know him personally, the only thing that mattered is that Papa Bear sent him and cosigned for him. When they got to the property that Papa Bear owned, they bounced side to side on the rough bumpy dirt road. The driver got to the opening entrance, and instead of parking at the house where Papa lived, the driver turned left and rode through another man-made dirt road.

Amil looked out the window, watching the thick pine trees and bushes pass by. The further they rode, the darker it seemed. Just up ahead, the driver stopped the SUV because the road ran out.

"What's out here?" she asked. "Papa's house is back there."

Fly looked at her, and at the same time, he placed his hand on the inside door latch. "Come on, you got some business to handle." He opened the door, picked his cane up from the floor and stepped out.

From the other side, Amil stepped out also and inhaled the fresh evening air. She looked through the windows of the SUV and saw Fly walking toward the front of the Yukon. She met him there. The driver sat patiently, and Fly and Amil walked through the bushes, pushing their way through a thin dirt trail.

Amil looked up at him. "Where we going?"

"I'm getting you prepared to take the throne," he said calmly.

That statement alone made her stare at him in total silence. She was definitely curious now, and was eagerly waiting to see what he had in store for her. For the next five minutes, they walked in silence through the thick woods.

Fly spotted a wooded stake that was nailed in the ground with a neon bright flag hanging from it. He made a left there, and walked further, moving some of the limbs out of the way with his cane. He spotted a solid oak wood box that stood about eight feet high, built on a slab of concrete. The entire set up looked like an outhouse from an old western movie.

Fly stopped, Amil did also. He went in his waistline and removed a small compact .380. To his left, there was a circular bulls eye attached to one of the trees. Fly handed Amil his cane. "Hold this."

She took the cane. He pulled the top of the gun back and loaded a bullet into the chamber. "Make sho' you pay close attention because you only get two practice runs okay."

Amil stared at him to see if he was actually serious. When she didn't respond, he looked at her. "You following me, Amil?"

She nodded her head. "I'm following you." she finally said.

Fly aimed the gun at the tree, his finger carefully on the trigger. When he pulled it, the gun roared and the shell casing jumped out and landed on the ground. Amil squinted her eyes and her heart raced. She was excited and anxious. Her mouth was beginning to water.

Fly walked behind her and she carefully sat the cane on the ground. Standing behind her, he put the gun in her hand, and his hands on top of hers. He made her aim at the bulls eye, then he made her put her index finger on the trigger.

"Pull the trigger."

Once again, Amil squinted her eyes. She squeezed the trigger, and the gun roared. Fly braced her for the impact. "Pull it again," he said into her ear.

She did.

"Again."

She did

"Again."

She did.

"Okay, Amil. I'ma step back and let you do it by yourself. Are you ready?" He removed his hands from hers and stepped to her side and picked up his cane.

Amil nodded her head. Both of her hands rested carefully on the rubber grip of the gun. She was still aiming at the bulls eye. "I'm ready."

"Pull the trigger," he said in a demanding voice. Standing next to her, he watched her eyes.

Amil pulled the trigger. The .380 jerked upward, but it didn't move her backwards. She was surprised that she could do it all by herself. When she smiled, she looked directly at Fly.

"Keep your eyes on the target, Amil. Always focus on the target."

# 36

Amil turned back toward the bulls eye and the smile quickly faded from her face. Her finger steady on the trigger, she found room to take a quick deep breath. "I'm ready," she whispered and braced herself even more.

"This time, focus on your aim." He pointed at the bulls eye. "Go."

Amil fired the .380 again and it cracked through the air. The bullet found the circle dead center. Fly smiled and clapped. "This the last practice round." He took the gun from her, removed the clip and replaced it with a full one.

"This is easier than I thought," she said, cheerfully.

"Definitely, all a piece of cake." He handed her the .380 again. "This time, I want you to empty the clip. That means you got to keep pulling that trigger until all the bullets are in the bulls eye."

Amil listened to his words carefully. Watching his eyes, she knew he was serious. She turned away from him and faced the bulls eye. Both hands wrapped around the grip. Her eyes squinted and she pulled the trigger. One. Two. Three. Four. Five. Six. Seven. Eight. Click, the gun locked back and smoke seeped from the barrel. The smell of gunpowder was thick in the air. She looked at Fly and gave him a serious stare.

He clapped his hands, and with a smile, he said, "I'm proud of you."

She looked at him and smiled in return. Fly gave her a hug and removed the gun from her hand. "See how easy that was?" he said. "Momma will be proud of you."

"Is that it?" she asked.

"That was just the practice run. We'll move on to the next phase."

She looked up at him. "What's the next phase?" She was anxious and over excited to the point that she began rubbing the palms of her hands together.

Fly removed another clip from his pocket and jammed it into the bottom of the .380. He turned toward the wooded box. "Bring him out Papa."

Just then, Papa Bear came from the back side of the small wooden box with Ox in shackles and hands cuffed behind his back. Ox was dressed in a camouflage colored jumpsuit and his head was covered with a black silk sack. Papa Bear walked him out to where Fly and Amil were standing.

He kicked the back of his legs and said calmly, "On your knees, stay there."

Ox went to his knees and Fly snatched the silk bag from his head and threw it to the ground. Amil looked at him. Her eyes went to Papa Bear, and he gave her a very serious look that she had never seen on him before.

"Pay attention, Amil." he said to her. "This is Ox, one of the dudes that were responsible for kidnapping you."

Amil looked at Ox long and hard. His head was up and he stared her dead in her eyes. Then he dropped his head, looking at the shell casings on the ground.

"What I need you to do, Amil, is take the gun and put two

bullets in the center of his forehead." He cocked the gun and handed it to her.

Amil didn't ask any questions. She received the .380. Her eyes went to Papa Bear and he slowly nodded his head up and down. She looked at Ox, and standing no more than two feet away from him, she took aim.

"Hold yo' muthafuckin' head up, nigga. Look at my sistah while she talk."

Slowly, Ox's head raised up and his eyes were half opened.

Amil's heart was thumping harder now, her palms turned sweaty, and she suddenly became nervous.

Fly noticed her hands trembling and said, "This is for your position on the throne, Amil. Go ahead. Two shots and we'll watch him die right here at our feet together."

Amil was panicky now, her throat was turning dry and her breathing was getting heavier and heavier. Twenty seconds passed and she still hadn't pulled the trigger. Her eyes cut to Papa Bear again. This time, he looked away from her. She looked at Fly. Beads of sweat had formed on her forehead.

"This is what we call leg work, Amil. This is the only way you can take the throne, Amil." His voice raised another notch. "Now put them two bullets in his damn head."

Amil took aim again, sweat poured from her face. The gun shook in her hand so bad that Fly took it from her. He looked at her. "What's the matter Amil?"

She whispered softly. "I can't."

"Fuck you mean, you can't? We don't use that word. You got to kill him now. Today. You wanna walk in your momma shoes? You wanna run this shit?" He moved close to her and stuffed the gun in her hand again. This time, he stood behind her but she forcefully wiggled out of his arm.

"Stop." she shouted at Fly.

Fly couldn't believe his ears. He saw Amil move closer towards Papa Bear. "Will you take me back to the hospital?"

"No." Fly shouted and began walking towards her. "You gon' kill this nigga today."

Amil turned toward Papa Bear and hugged him. Her face buried in his chest and she started crying. "Tell him to leave me alone."

Papa Bear looked at Fly and motioned his hand for him to slow down. Fly stopped, a smile appeared over his face and he toned his voice down. "You want me to do it? Turn around, watch your big brother work."

"Please take me back to my mother," she said to Papa Bear. She was trying her best to ignore her brother.

"Okay, fine. We'll keep him until you ready to kill him." Fly turned away from Papa Bear and Amil.

He picked up the silk bag from the ground and placed it back on Ox's head. "Stand up," Fly told him.

Ox rose to his feet and Fly personally walked him back to the wooden box, took him around to the door, pushed him inside and locked it with the steel bolt. Fly laughed to himself as he walked back around to where Papa Bear and Amil stood. Without another word amongst the three of them, they loaded inside the Yukon.

Fly rode in the front while Amil and Papa took the back seat. "Back to the hospital." Fly said.

# 37

Nearly three more weeks passed and Falisa still hadn't come out of her coma. As usual, Amil and Iris were there with her every day. Pepé flew in and out of town to check on her, usually at night when no one else was there. It was difficult for him to see her so lifeless, but he had complete faith in the medical professionals that were taking care of her. He was aware of the hostility that her family quietly held for him, so he tried to keep a low profile.

Over the course of the last three weeks, Amil had developed a deep hatred for her brother. Her mind was more focused on him than anything else in her life. They hadn't spoken since that terrible day. She had used her 'SHUT DOWN' technique, and did not speak to anyone, except Falisa.

Amil rubbed the side of her mother's face and began whispering in her ear. "If you would talk to me, I would know what direction to take. But since you're refusing me, Mother, I must go ahead with my own decision."

Amil sat there for a minute, then she stood up. Dressed casually in a two-piece pants suit and Michael Kors heels that she borrowed from her mother's wardrobe, she walked over to where Iris was sitting.

"What's wrong?" Iris asked her.

Amil leaned over and kissed Iris' cheek. "I'm going downstairs. Want me to bring you something back?"

"Hawaiian Punch." She went back to reading her newspaper.

Amil walked out the door and into the lobby area. There was a row of payphones on the wall. She picked up the first one and dropped a quarter into it. She punched a number and it began to ring.

On the fourth ring, Smurf answered. "Hello."

"Hey Smurf, this Amil."

"Hey Amil. What's wrong?"

"Nothing. Why do you ask?"

"You never called me before, that's all."

"I thought this was the family emergency number. I was looking for my brother."

"Here's a direct number to him. Four zero four, nine six eight. Twelve thirty-two."

Without a thank you or anything, she calmly hung up the phone and dialed the operator.

ON THE THIRTY-THIRD floor of the Ritz-Carlton Residences in the Buckhead neighborhood of Atlanta, Fly was lying naked on his bed sipping champagne straight from the bottle. He was on overload with pain pills that made him feel drowsy and lazy. Zoë was lying next to him, naked. Her body gently curved, and he was tripping off an old episode of Martin where he kicked Pam out of their apartment.

His cell phone rang. He knew it was Smurf, because no one else had his number. He removed it from the night stand and pressed the send button. "What's up, brah?" he asked in a low deep tone.

"This isn't brah, this is your sister, Fly." Amil responded in a sassy manner.

He didn't seem concerned at all. He turned up his champagne bottle, Zoë turned over, and the first thing she did was grab his penis underneath the covers.

"Mama out the coma?" He asked, hoping that was her reason for calling.

"Not yet, she probably will be soon, though."

"You must know something I don't."

"As a matter of fact, I do. And I just can't keep it a secret any longer."

Fly became curious. He moved his dreads away from his face and sat up a little. "What's the secret, Amil?" He swiped away Zoë's hand.

"It's about your so called fiancé, Zoë. You know that bitch was gonna have you robbed, but Mother interfered and stopped it without you even knowing anything about it. That bitch wasn't going to Spelman when you met her. The bitch ain't from nowhere near Missouri, and the bitch parents isn't in the fucking military. I know you don't believe me, but you better. All you got to do is ask her. She gonna tell the truth, cause she'll think Mother told you. That's all. And I love you, okay. I'm sure you'll handle business."

She hung up.

Fly laid there in silence for the next five minutes, his mind racing. He kept replaying the conversation with Amil in his head. He slowly sat his phone down on the nightstand and stared at the Martin show on the TV screen. *Damn!* He said to himself.

He turned over and faced Zoë. Her face was beautiful and outlined with jet-black hair. Fly rubbed the side of her face, and then leaned toward her and kissed her. When her lips meet his, she felt a sharp pain on the back of her neck. He pinched her hard enough to make her say 'ouch'.

Then Fly said in the calmest voice, "My sources are telling me that you and my mama have a secret that you wish to share with me. But first, before you say anything, if you lie to me, I'ma kill yo' ass. Bottom line."

*Zoë's eyes were on his and Falisa words were etched into her brain.* You got to take this one to the grave, sweetheart. Fly is indeed my son, and on my word, I'll never tell him about this, and neither will Iris. *She would never forget that statement.*

"I got behind on my studies at school, and she got a tutor for me. That's it." Zoë lied smoothly, but her heart was burning with fear.

Fly kissed her lips again, and quickly laid his hand on her chest. He stayed calm and still, while her heart felt like it was about to leap through her flesh and bones, Fly came to the conclusion that she was either lying or scared. He sat up and turned away from her.

Fly sat on the side of the bed and he strapped on his prosthesis in a calm manner, and then he stood and wrapped himself in a white robe.

"Where are you going?" Zoë asked as she eased over to his side of the bed.

Fly turned around quickly, clutched a fist full of her hair, and yanked her head backwards. "Whhhyyy? Stop." Zoë yelled.

Fly poured champagne in her face. "You lying." Animosity was in his voice. Then, without another word, he smashed the bottle across her face and forehead. She yelled out in pain.

"Shut up." He limped with her and headed toward the outside balcony, leaving a trail of blood on the carpet as he went. When he got to the glass entrance of the balcony, he stopped and looked at her. "On my word. If you tell me the truth, I'll let you live. If you lie, you gonna jump thirty-three floors down. Even a cat won't land on his feet."

"I promise you."

"Was it your plan to have me robbed?"

"No."

Fly's robe was open and he had blood on his sleeve. He gripped her hair tighter and opened the sliding door. When he pulled her out, her breasts were bouncing and now she began fighting for her life. Fly was naturally strong in his entire upper body and one leg. He lifted her with both hands, and she began screaming and holding on to his dreads for dear life. With all his strength, he tossed her over.

He stood there and looked over the balcony, trying to see where she landed. His heart was now racing. He turned around and snatched the robe off, and then dropped it in a shopping bag. When he got back to the bedroom to get dressed, there was a knock at the door. Fly looked over his shoulder, a panicky look was in his eyes. *Who the fuck knocking at my door?* He asked himself.

BOOM! BOOM! BOOM!

The knocks had turned louder. It sounded like the police to Fly. He stood up. "Just a minute," he said.

Fly went to his closet and pulled out his folded wheelchair. He unfolded it, then he snatched a sheet from the bed and tried to spread it across the floor to cover the blood stains. Time was against him. He sat down in the chair naked, removed his prosthesis and eased it underneath the bed. Then he grabbed the cordless phone and rolled through his apartment. He got to the front door and began to unlock it while dialing 911 on the phone.

When he opened the door, there were two uniformed officers standing there with weapons drawn and pointed directly at him. He didn't pay them any attention and spoke into the phone. "Yes ma'am, a lady just jumped from the roof. Wait, it's some officers here now." Fly dropped the phone from his face, and when he looked up at the officers, he tried his acting skills by making a worried face appear. "I'm talking to 911 now, officers. And I was telling her that somebody just jumped from somewhere upstairs."

The front officer scanned over Fly's naked body and noticed that he only had one leg. "But we got a call about a disturbance from this residence."

"Wrong apartment, sir. I'm handicapped as you can see, and I was just getting out the tub."

The front officer looked undecided. He turned to his partner. "Call for back-up, and go upstairs. I'll take a look around in here." He looked at Fly. "Sir, can you cover yourself up?"

The officer in the rear took off running toward the stairs and talking on his radio at the same time. Without consent, the front officer pushed himself inside Fly's apartment and began looking around. Fly turned his wheelchair around and rolled in behind him. *If they got a call to my spot, Amil must've sent them.* He thought to himself.

Fly grabbed a towel while the officer looked around. When Fly saw him go toward the balcony, he headed toward the door in his wheelchair.

Fly opened the door, and the officer yelled, "Freeze, don't you muthafuckin' move."

Fly was down bad. He didn't have a weapon, and he didn't have his leg on. If he did, he would've run like hell. When he felt the barrel of the gun pressing against the back of his head, all he could do was raise his hands high above his head. *Damn. Amil, my own sister set me up.*

# 38

Eight days later, Falisa came out of her coma. When she managed to open her eyes, they were drained and tired looking. The first words that registered in her mind were from Amil. "Hey Mother." she whispered softly in her ear.

Falisa still couldn't move. Her neck was wrapped in a six-inch foam and plastic neck brace. She shifted her eyes toward Amil, and when she saw her face, she managed a small smile. "Hey, baby." Falisa barely whispered.

Amil grabbed Falisa's hand, brought it up to her lips and kissed the back of it. "I'm here with you," she whispered, then a tear fell down her cheek. She leaned in closer to Falisa's face. "You had me worried to the point that I've lost eight pounds in the last thirty days."

"Well, you can stop worrying now." Falisa words were only coming in a low and soft tone. Then she managed to ask. "Where's Fly?"

Amil gave her mother a very disappointed look. "Fly has gotten himself in a little trouble. He turned to drugs, Mother, when you went into a coma. Then, for no reason at all," she paused and took a deep breath. "He killed his fiancé, Zoë, in Atlanta."

"Where is he?" Her eyes turned moist, then she batted them.

"He's in Fulton County jail. They're holding him without a bond. Trust me on this, he's okay. However, on the business side of things, I opened up a couple of new accounts with Pepé's help. Your offshore Switzerland account has five million secured safely, in an untraceable account. Our South Dakota trust fund has five hundred thousand in it, and we made an agreement with the bankers that we wouldn't touch it for at least thirty-six months. I definitely couldn't resist the Caribbean offshore account. We put in a million and Pepé put in three. Yesterday, I set us up for Dubai bank also. They'll contact me in seven days after all the paperwork is processed. Also, since Fly couldn't hold his position on the throne, I put myself in charge until you are capable of taking it back.

"Smurf isn't talking to me, because for some reason or another, he thinks I'm responsible for Fly being locked up." She waved her hand dismissively and went on. "He is still handling Georgia and the Carolinas. Iris picks up all the Alabama money and Papa is back in New York again. Pig Man calls every day to check up on you. That's all."

After Amil finished talking, Falisa laid there in pure silence for the next few minutes. Then she whispered, "I'm proud of you. The throne is yours until I say otherwise."

Casually, Amil kissed the back of her mother's hand again, and then her forehead. "A real queen always makes the wisest decisions," she said softly. "Thank you, Mother, I won't let you down."

~

When Falisa finished telling the nurse the rest of the story, she was sitting at the table with her mouth parted open and staring at Falisa in pure amazement. Nearly two hours had passed, and the nurse couldn't believe what she had just heard. "Damn! Now that was deep." She pulled a few sheets of Kleenex from the box and wiped her eyes. "A horse, you fell off a damn horse?"

There was a small silence, then Falisa said, "Yeah, and out of all things a muthafuckin' snake bit the horse that I was riding."

"What a coincidence." The nurse responded.

"Yeah it was. But in my heart, I feel like that snake's soul was connected to Timbo's bitch ass."

"Wow," The nurse said in a slow drawl. "So what happened when you came out the coma?"

"I'm sure you couldn't digest the rest of this story. You cried three times already. That's enough for today."

The nurse could do nothing but shake her head in a disgusted manner. Her luminous brown eyes stared directly at Falisa. "Please don't tell me, another cliffhanger."

Falisa poured herself a shot of Courvoisier XO Imperial and downed it quickly. The warmth from the alcohol warmed her insides in seconds.

She smiled at the nurse. "Of course," she whispered. Then she added, "But trust me darling, it'll be worth the wait."

## A NOTE FROM COLE HART

As you know, no one comes before God in my book. Now allow me to thank my wife and my kids for their ongoing support. My family that's been supporting me since I've been incarcerated. Thank you. Allow me to recognize my incarcerated homies and brothers that have been supporting me in here when I have been determined to make you listen at my stories all day. I'm not interested in boring the audience, so let me get this out real quick. Carl Pig Sloan, Marco Appling, Chedo Tanksley, John Mack, Ronnie Overton, Marquette Larry, Bertram Scarface Owens, Dooly Overstreet, Lorenzo Lindsey, Kelvin Prince, Michael Big Maine Ward, Carl Coleman. The homie Levi (Duncan Blocc), Carlos Grier, Gangsta Dre(WSGC), Xavier Womack (SGC) practicing Muslim. Oh man I can go on forever with this list. Isaiah McCoy, my Lil homie C Boss, Ronald Coleman. I can't call out everyone, in all honesty. To my homies, comrades and warriors whose names I didn't mention, don't worry, this is definitely not my last book, so I'll keep it rotating. And if your name is spelled wrong by a letter or something. You know who you are.

Now, for the circle that I'm constantly working with every

day. My CEO D.Weave, brah you gonna definitely have to cover me on this one cause I'm going in for real. Honestly, I'm more dangerous with a pen than a K any day. They must've thought I was playing when I was saying we were gonna win this Championship. Ballin' so hard lames in the nosebleed section is blowing their whistles. And they ain't even no referees. How they do that? And for those of you that don't know what the letters #TBRS stand for. It's Team Bank Roll Squad, we probably about 10,000 deep just in case you wanted to know. I'm not flexing about no numbers because one thing we all know for sure is that they don't lie.

To Tremayne, Torica, Shan, Alicia, Chanel and Envy. Y'all know what we got to do. Let's take this game by storm. And the only way we can do that is by giving the world this WERK. To my editor, Tina Nance, thanks for bringing this one through a successful surgery for me. My home girl Karen Cummings. Thanks for reppin' #TBRS. Man, a big stupid shout out to our immediate reading group and circle. I salute you. And once again, I know I left someone out. Eureka Oliver keep grinding. Keep writing. RIP to Leo Lamont Utley. If you from that AUG you know who this man is. Paying Homage.

P.S, I was supposed to have put my own personal Obituary Section in this book for one author in particular, however. I won't call your name because I was told to leave the dead dead. But for the record ...I know what you did last summer ... and it wasn't no book sales. So gone with the games homie... Get Right.

## AN AMERICAN HUSTLER

I never had intentions to become a drug dealer, especially at the age of thirteen--just being honest. I had one of the meanest mamas in the neighborhood, who made me go to church almost every Sunday. I had to sang in the Jr. Choir, I'd been baptized, and was a member of a church called Williams Memorial CME on Fifteenth Street. Just across the street is where I stood in line, faithfully, at Shiloe Community Center for our free cheese, powdered milk, honey and most importantly, our monthly Food Stamps.

I wanted to be a football player growing up, but for some apparent reason, my mama didn't think I was tough enough or that I would get hurt. While growing up in a poverty-stricken city such as Augusta, and living in one of the worst neighborhoods, you had only a few options. Either you was going to be a boxer, play football, or be a damn good hustler. Even though the city had produced a few NBA players and rappers, your chances were still slim to none.

Still, I never had intentions on being a drug dealer. I was doing just fine drawing pictures of cartoon characters on my bedroom wall. I was obsessed with picking up soda and beer cans and selling them at the aluminum recycle company on Old Savannah Road. We hunted squirrels and robins with BB guns and sold them to the lady down the street for a dollar. That was my hustle, I guess.

My intentions on being a drug dealer were nonexistent, but this would be the last time our lights and the water would be disconnected at almost simultaneously. I was sure my mama was oblivious to what I was going through mentally. In school, I was ridiculed for various reasons; going to school musty, wearing hand me down clothes that my Mama had gotten from the rich white people that she worked for on the Hill, I also got joked on by the older guys in my neighborhood because they said that my mama didn't know who my daddy was. Maybe, all of this had taken a toll on me.

Then, one day, something clicked mentally; almost similar to someone flipping on a light switch on the wall… And from there, all I could remember is my mama saying, *Whatever you do, just be the best at it.*

This is a powerful story of drug addiction, redemption of overcoming the life of crime and the judicial system all together, Jarvis Hardwick AKA National Bestselling author, Cole Hart, has finally pinned a riveting and unputdownable story of his life

**Coming Soon…**

Made in the USA
Columbia, SC
10 December 2024

48945698R00126